About the Author

Tim Penny was born and raised in Hampshire. He went to UCL, a university in Preston where he discovered his love of storytelling and started writing. In recent years he has worked his way up in the TV industry to the position of producer/director, where he has made a number of documentary and factual series for the BBC, ITV and Channel 4. He currently lives in Surrey with his wife, Camilla, and their puppy, Rosie.

You Betrayed Us

Tim Penny

You Betrayed Us

Olympia Publishers
London

www.olympiapublishers.com
OLYMPIA PAPERBACK EDITION

A CIP catalogue record for this title is
available from the British Library.

ISBN: 978-1-80074-580-3

First Published in 2023

Olympia Publishers
Tallis House
2 Tallis Street
London
EC4Y 0AB

Printed in Great Britain

Dedication

I dedicate this book to my wife, Camilla, for the countless walks and evenings spent discussing the plot and encouraging me to write this book.

Acknowledgements

Special thanks to Mum, Dad and Sarah for their support. Also, thanks to the ambulance and the crew– Orlaigh, Emily and Leon. Where I wrote the majority of this book, while shooting a TV series.

Prologue

The cold air feels like daggers on his face as he makes his way towards the restaurant; winter has fully descended on the city now. He should have brought a scarf, or at least better gloves. He has chosen a restaurant that he thinks is a safe option for a first date – nice Italian not too fancy but not too cheap either, hitting the spot just right. Thoughts racing through his head at a million miles an hour as he walks closer and closer. He is so nervous. He hasn't felt this nervous since he was twenty-five years old when he was waiting at the top of the aisle for his beloved to come through the doors. If he had known then what he knows now he wouldn't have been so nervous, he wouldn't have been there at all.

Cutting down an alleyway that he knows is a short cut although it has its reputation, he feels fairly safe but wants to get there early and get settled as this is the first date he has had since the incident. He needs a moment, it's taken him a while to get out there but with his mates, including his ex-brother-in-law, finally wearing him down, he conceded to joining a dating site. Jennifer, that's her name, she was the first person that replied to his messages. She was the same age as him, nice blond hair, same tastes... He was pleasantly surprised after constantly being told of dating horror stories. He walks in and introduces himself to the waiter, who shows him to his table, he peruses the menu before she arrives because he is awful at decision making and doesn't want to come across as a dithering idiot. There she is. Right on time.

She looks even more beautiful than her profile pic. He gets up and introduces himself and pulls the chair out for her and makes sure she is comfortable. The next two hours fly by, she's laughing at all of his jokes, touching his arm and smiling with that twinkle in her eye. They have a lovely meal and he wonders why he spent the last two days worrying about it so much. As they put on their coats, she puts on a big thick knit beanie, which she looks absolutely phenomenal in. He's not sure what she expects ... a hug, a kiss, a formal handshake. He is so inexperienced at this. He goes for the hug which seems to be the right approach and he says they must do this again some time and they arrange to see each other again at the same time next week. He is absolutely jumping for joy inside but remains composed as they say their goodbyes. He starts walking back to the car and now the cold air doesn't seem so bad. It's almost pleasant. He goes a different way back enjoying the walk and not taking the shortcut. As he is walking, he gets a text from his ex-brother-in-law asking, "How did the date go, dude?" As he is replying he suddenly hears a deathly scream break out in the clear crisp night. Normally he would think it was teenagers mucking about or some drunken group on their way to the next pub but this seemed different. As he turns back towards where the scream came from, he heads back towards the short cut he took earlier. Turning the corner, he sees something on the floor and he squints his eyes to try and make out what it is in the poor light. He slowly approaches and the shape becomes ever clearer. It's a body.

He reaches down apprehensively and touches them. There is no response. He notices a strand of blonde hair under a thick knit beanie, and then everything goes black and a faint sound of sirens can be heard approaching.

Chapter 1

The last few hours have been an absolute blur; stress is what the doctor called it. Rupert is still trying to get his mind around what has happened. He thought it was his imagination playing tricks when he walked down the alleyway and seeing the body lying there. The police turned up before he could do anything. The next thing Rupert remembered is being checked in at the police station and the big police guard whose job it is to sign every criminal into the station. The sort of man who couldn't really give a shit if you had just robbed a shop or been caught on a serial killer spree. "Name," he says with no emotion.

"Rupert."

He looks back.

"No, your full name, I need it to check you in."

"Rupert Graham," he says with a heavy voice.

The two policemen standing either side of Rupert don't look at him, treating him like an animal. It's just routine, he says to himself. "Address?" As he brings him back into the room.

"Flat 9, High Street, Winchester, SO23 6GH," he resumes back to the screen. "Right lads put him in a cell, second on the left," he says. The two policemen grab each of Rupert's arms and pretty much drag him to the cell. The doctor was then called to make sure Rupert was cognitive and did the standard drug and blood test. Time is dragging. Two hours feel more like six.

Rupert can see the light starting to change through the tiny box window in his cell. It must be early morning. Rupert's heart rate has been going like crazy lying on this uncomfortable bed, thoughts racing through his head. He can't stop them. The little flap opens on the cell door and a gruff shout of "breakfast" comes through the door. His back spasms as he gets off the bed. He thinks that he should have done more at the gym instead of letting his life fall away the last six months. As Rupert approaches the door, he sees what looks like re-heated mash and the milkiest cup of tea you've ever seen. "Excuse me, when am I going to be seen?" Rupert asks through the hole.

It's met with a gruff shout, "When they are ready."

The shout seems to disturb the other cell inhabitants, shouts of, "Fucking pigs are never ready" and "Where's my lawyer?" ring down the hallway. Looking at the four stark grey walls of the cell, Rupert starts to eat his breakfast.

Chapter 2

Detective Chief Inspector Jessica Spears is just arriving into work at 5.45 a.m. for her early shift, she had to sneak out of the house this morning hoping not to wake up her mother and baby. She is sure Joseph gets fed up with her working so much but since her mum is on disability benefits, she is the only one bringing in decent money to support them all, plus she loves her job. She has always been a career minded person and even with the struggle of getting into the police force with her past, she has risen up the ranks and recently been made lead detective after working on the ground for many years. She does her normal morning routine walking past the reception and making sure she says good morning to everybody. With these early shifts she knows the importance of keeping everybody's spirits up.

As she arrives to her floor, she says good morning to her team and walks into the office to make a coffee. She steals a moment for herself before the manic day begins. She is halfway through her coffee when there is a knock on the door. "And so, it begins," she thinks to herself a she gestures for them to come in. David, the newest member of the team, wants to impress her so is always on the ball. "That will change," she thinks, "once he gets into the swing of things."

David enters carrying a file. "What can I do for you, David?" Jessica asks.

"A case came in late last night that I think you should have a look at before the briefing, Ma'am."

Jessica rolls her eyes. "David what have I told you? You don't have to greet me as Ma'am, Jess is absolutely fine."

David looks a bit sheepish, he is only junior but she has always wanted to be the boss that everyone can talk to without the formalities. "Sorry Maa ... Jess."

"So, what is so important about this case that it can't wait until the briefing," Jess asks.

David looks as his file and starts getting out the papers. "So late last night we got an anonymous 999 call saying that they feared for a woman's safety. They had seen a man acting suspiciously towards a woman in a restaurant and thought something might happen. They last saw her walking towards Barber Alley, you know the alleyway that is between the two barbers in town. It's quite a long one and often used as a short cut, so obviously we sent out a patrol car with blues on to just to do the rounds and scare anyone off. When the two officers arrived, they found a man slumped over a young blonde girl." Jess is listening thinking of all the scenarios that it could be, what she didn't want to hear is what came out David's mouth next "She was dead ... We have brought the man into custody and he is currently in a holding cell awaiting interview."

"Okay," Jessica says. "Can I have a look at the file?" She reaches her hand across as David hands the piece of paper over. She glances over it reading, "Name: Rupert Graham, clean record, no previous convictions." She noticed that Mr Rupert Graham had never even been caught speeding. "Why didn't you think that this could wait until the briefing?" She could guess the answer.

"Because I thought you would want to get started on this case straight away. It's an odd case, no previous convictions and suddenly out of the blue he kills a girl he has been on one date with." That's not what she thought he would say, "and that you have a famous track record with these cases." Ah, there it is, she thought her past record always seems to be what everybody mentions. It happened almost five years ago when there was a case of a number of unsolved murders that all came in separately with almost no connection between them all. The case made national news and was quoted to be "unsolvable". Everyone within the force had pretty much written the case off but Jess managed to find the tiniest bit of evidence which linked all of them to this baker who was identifying the victims when they came into his shop. She became a headline name for a week and got promoted. Ever since, everybody thinks she can solve every tricky case there is.

She looks at the file again, she didn't know what she was looking for but she had the feeling that there was something they were missing. "Okay, get the suspect ready for IV and make sure he has a lawyer present, I don't want anything being misunderstood that can mean this case falls flat, okay?"

"Yes Jess, what do you want me to do about the morning briefing?"

"Make it in five minutes, I want everybody out there so we can get them working on the case before the interview."

Chapter 3

I can't believe it's actually happened after so much planning. It took meticulous timing to make that happen for you to be in the right place and I was so close to being caught, a second or two later and then it would have all fallen apart. It took months to find the correct moment and then it came. I couldn't believe my luck. Do I feel guilty for taking a young woman's life? I did for a fleeting moment but then it actually felt a relief, like a burning inside of me that was waiting to get out. I had a moment of clarity that I was doing it all for the right reasons, to get justice. I was surprised by how easy it was. When I first grabbed her and held her to the floor, but I didn't think she would scream as loud as she did. Then a couple of minutes later I was watching her life slip away from her, she looked so scared just waiting to die, but her part in this story was over. It was only fleeting but it served a purpose – it enabled me to get to you. Is that cruel? Most will say yes but for me, I can't tell you how much I have dreamed of this.

I got a huge thrill from it, I even risked everything by standing nearby not expecting to see anything but what I do see and what fills me with joy is the image of you approaching and finding the body. I didn't plan on that, it just happened naturally. The original plan was to call nearby and explain I had seen someone matching your description running from the scene, but I didn't have to do that anymore. With you stood over her I took my chance and made the call on the burner phone I bought ages ago when I had started thinking of a way to get to you. I put on a show speaking to the police and making it sound like I was a concerned citizen who had watched a poor defenceless woman just get brutally attacked and I was so struck with fear there was nothing I could do.

It doesn't matter now though, it's happened and my plan is finally coming to fruition. Let's hope that I have done enough to make you pay for what you did.

Chapter 4

Finally, after what seems like hours, although it's probably only been about thirty minutes. There is a jangle of keys and the door creaks open. The sergeant that checked Rupert in earlier says, "Mr. Graham, please will you follow me?" Rupert thinks that there has been some sort of mistake and stands up and start to walk towards the door past him, but the guard sticks his arm across and says, "Hands out". Rupert obliges and feels the coldness of the cuffs being clicked back on his wrists. He walks behind him down the long corridor while the other people who are in the cells bang and scream begging to be let out or insisting they haven't done anything.

Being brought out in to the main room he is led to a phone and told to call a lawyer. "Do I really need a lawyer?"

The guard turns and eyeballs Rupert. "Look," he says, "I would get a lawyer, I know you protest your innocence, but I'm not being funny so does everyone else. A lawyer is the only thing standing between you and us, and if you have or haven't done this, you need someone in your corner". He picks up the phone and hands it to him and walks away.

"Thank you," Rupert rasps. The guard doesn't respond, he just walks back to his desk and waits for the call to finish.

It's not a very long phone call to the lawyer. It's his ex-brother-in-law, Jason, who is a highly esteemed criminal lawyer. Rupert didn't ever think he'd be grateful to have someone in the business in the family. Jason tells him to sit tight and he will come down to the station. "Don't say anything. Don't worry this will all be resolved as a misunderstanding." His voice doesn't match his words. The odds aren't exactly in favour of Rupert, found crouched over a dead body, doesn't exactly do wonders for an argument of innocence. After the phone call, Rupert is taken back to his cell. The sergeant doesn't say a word to him as he leads Rupert back into his cell and locks the door. Once again Rupert is back looking at the four walls.

Chapter 5

"So, thank you for meeting a bit earlier than we normally do. The reason that we have gathered is because a case came in last night at 2300 hours." She turns towards her trusty white board, she can see some of the information left over from the last case that was written on the board, a burglary of a jewellery store in town, she wishes that was the case she was about to write. She's got a feeling that once she writes it on the board it's going to be a long time before she writes another one. She starts writing as she is talking out loud.

"So, what we have is," she writes the name down: Jennifer Green, and circles it in a red circle "Jennifer Green. She went on a date with…" with this she writes down Rupert Graham, this time she circles it with a black circle. "Rupert Graham, they have a date at Giuseppe's, the Italian restaurant in town." She draws a line between them. "However, this is not an ordinary date as Jennifer ends up dead four hours later down Barber Alley. Rupert is found leaning over her." She now writes VICTIM and next to Rupert's name, she writes SUSPECT. "What our job is to find out what happened between them arriving at the restaurant and Jennifer's death. We are currently waiting for a full coroner's report to confirm time and type of death, but we are pretty sure she was strangled." She looks at her team, each and every one of them in the eye. "So, I want you guys to split into three teams." She writes three headings of Alpha, Bravo and Charlie and then details each job out on the board. "So Alpha," she says as she's writing down the names, "that's James and David. I want you guys to go and talk to the restaurant and trawl the CCTV from them. I want everything scrutinised and want to have screen shots of any inappropriate behaviour that Rupert did towards Jennifer. Did she seem upset or uncomfortable at any point in the evening? How was the date left? I want every body movement, every smile, every look, you name it. I want to see it."

"Got it, boss," James replied from the back.

"Bravo, That's Ava and John. I want you to go through their backgrounds to see if there is anything suspicious about either of them, for all we know Jennifer had an ex-lover that had a score to settle. Remember, like Team Alpha, I want everything, no stone unturned, got it?"

"Yes boss," shouts Ava. Jess knows that she can be a bit of a control freak when it comes to cases, she always has been, everything has got to be right. Her team knows that.

"Team Charlie, that's Olivia and Isabella. I want witness statements from anyone in the vicinity of the murder scene, I want to know if they have CCTV, if they heard anything, saw anything okay?"

"Absolutely," came the reply from the team.

"Brilliant, thanks everyone. We'll reconvene as soon as we can and see what we have come up with. I will be interviewing Mr Graham in the next hour so if you find anything come and tell me. I have an open-door policy, please don't hesitate to use it" She walks back into her office to prepare for the IV and read over the notes to check that she is ready. She has to be ready. She needs to solve this case, whatever the outcome.

Chapter 6

Rupert who has been pacing his cell trying to get his head around what has happened in the last twenty-four hours, occasionally stopping whenever footsteps are near the door. Rupert is thinking back to last year when he and Steph were married, living in the house they always wanted and getting ready to take their third holiday of the year. He and Steph both worked in the television industry and were both producers working in different genres, which worked for them it meant they were always working on different things. Rupert always joked how nice that was as it would be hell if they ever got to work together, even though they worked really long hours and were often away on location for weeks on end. It was easy because they understood the work and they always came back together. They had been together on and off since they were fifteen, proper childhood sweethearts and he knew her family really well. Her brother was his best man at their wedding and her mum always called him an extra son, He just wished it hadn't ended like it did.

His thoughts are disrupted when he hears a key put in the lock of his cell door. The guard that had let him out earlier is stood there once again. 'Mr Graham, step forward please.' As Rupert steps forward, he puts his hands out this time automatically and the guard immediately places the cold handcuffs on his hands and drags him out of the cell. As he walks down the corridor, he has a slight flutter of hope. He thinks if he can just get in front of someone and tell his story then they have to believe him. They just have to. The guard stops them by a door that has a little metal plaque which reads Interview Room One.

As the door opens, Rupert sighs with relief as he sees Jason is sitting there waiting for him in his standard shirt jacket combo and heavy-set glasses. The guard grabs his wrists and releases the handcuffs. Rupert rubs his wrists and makes his way towards the chair that is next to Jason. "Am I glad to see you, mate," he says and Jason stands up and gives him a handshake

"Absolutely not a problem, mate, are you okay? You look terrible."

"I've had better days," Rupert replies with a bit of chuckle. Jason turning to the officer. "Please can we have the room I would like to speak to my client in private."

The officer, who looks a bit put out, turns and leaves. "Right," Jason says getting an A4 note pad out of his bag and grabbing a pen out of his top pocket, "tell me everything and I mean everything that happened."

Jess checks her watch, grabs the file that David left with her earlier. As she walks through the office, she shouts over to Andrew, her number two, "Are you ready for the interview? I could use a bit of that Andrew magic on this one." Jess and Andrew have worked together for the last ten years and they have never fallen out since they got paired together. She has the utmost faith in him and trusts him explicitly.

"Be right with you," he shouts. Jess can still spot the odd balloon dotted around the office from Andrew's fortieth she helped organise for him at the office. Jess checks her phone while she's waiting —There's a text from her mum saying the girls went to school just fine and she hope Jess's day is okay. She starts replying when Andrew interrupts her, "Sorry Jess I was just booking a restaurant for tonight. I've got a date."

"A date!" Jess replies. "Do tell more," and she gestures down the hallway. "Well, she's in the ambulance service and we met on that app, you know where service people meet?"

"That's amazing! I'm so pleased for you. You deserve to get back out there. Where are you going? Please don't tell me you're taking her to the Jade Palace!"

"Of course."

"Oh, Andrew why do you keep going to that place? You have got food poisoning every single time you've been there. I know Ubers with a better hygiene rating. I'll give you some recommendations after we have sorted this interview."

"Well, I think it's a nice place and great for a first date, if they can survive the Jade Palace then they are the girl for me," Andrew responds.

"Are you ready?" Jess says,

Andrew nods and they enter the interview room.

Chapter 7

Rupert hears the door open and looks up to see two officers walking into the room, one a woman with brown hair tied up into a tight bun and a man with grey hair. "Hello," the woman says as she sits down opposite. The grey-haired man turns on the police recording device and nods to the woman.

"Right, let's get started, shall we? For the purposes of the recording the officers in attendance are Detective Chief Inspector Jessica Spears and Detective Inspector Andrew Powell and for the recording can you confirm your full name please?"

"Rupert David Graham," he says, as he watches her getting her pen ready and shuffling a thin file with his name across the side.

"Excellent, thank you, Rupert, and can I ask who is here representing you?'"

Jason adjusts his glasses and leans forward

"Jason Isaacs. I am Mr Graham's attorney and will be representing him today."

"Okay well let's get started then, so Rupert can you please in your own words take us through your movements last night"

Rupert takes a deep breath and looks at Jason who nods.

"So, I met this girl through Tinder about three days ago and we chatted, you know, the usual." He holds his hands up in an air quote. "How long have you been single? Have you had much success on this? If you could be any animal what would you be? You know, that sort of thing, and we hit it off or I thought we did so I asked her out for a date."

"And how did she seem to take being asked for a date?" Jess asks.

"Yeah, pretty well, I think. We went through a couple of potential dates and eventually settled on last night and I decided to take her to one of my favourite restaurants, which was the Italian just on the High Street and she said she liked pizza so I thought it would be the perfect choice."

"Was there anything said in those messages that could have cause offence maybe create tension between you two?"

"Not that I know of. As far as I am aware everything was above board and she was happy and seemed excited."

"Are you sure because we are running checks on your phone right now and it would be better for everyone involved if you just told us now."

Rupert looks a bit uncomfortable, Jess notes, as he slowly shakes his head. "Okay then," Jess says, "so what happened at the dinner?"

"Well I arrived at the restaurant..."

"What time was this?" Andrew asks with pen ready at his notepad. Rupert looking across at Andrew.

"It was about seven-ish I think." Andrew jots down seven, and Rupert sees him circle it three times.

"Please continue," Jess says.

"I arrived at seven-ish. She wasn't there yet so I waited outside and checked my phone, browsed the internet a bit. You know check in with the Daily Mail, look at what's going on. She turned up after around five minutes and I quickly put my phone away, I gave her a quick hug and said shall we go inside."

"And how did she seem?" Jess adds.

"She seemed fine, a bit nervous but it was the first date that

28

we had both been on for a while, so it was understandable."

Andrew looks at Rupert. "Can you elaborate please?"

"Well, we had both previously had long-term partners and had both been burned in the past. We were trying to get back into the dating scene."

"Can you tell us how your divorce came about?"

"What does that have to do with anything?" Rupert asks.

"From where I'm sitting it could have everything to do with it," Jess replies.

"I would rather not discuss it."

"This is a criminal investigation, Rupert. We need you to answer our questions so we can either rule you out as a suspect or charge you."

"You can't possibly think I have anything to do with this."

"Well, you tell me, Rupert. What happened with your first wife?" Jess asks again. Poking the bruise that she's clearly found.

Jason interjects. "I think Mr Graham has made it perfectly clear that he doesn't want to talk about it and it's not relevant to the night in question." Jess writes down marriage with a big question mark after it.

"Okay, I think it is a relevant line of questioning as it shows how you perceive women, if you trust them at all? But anyway, we shall come back to it. So please Rupert continue, what happened next?"

Chapter 8

While the interview is going on back at the station. John and David, Team Alpha, are on their way to the restaurant to interview the witness. David's driving as he has on countless occasions been scared for his life while John was behind the wheel. David looks over at John who always makes him feel so old. David is a bit of dinosaur when it comes to the station, he's seen it all and done it all and is just clinging on until he is ready to retire. He's been offered it several times and constantly feels as though the boot is well and truly on his back. By comparison, John is a newbie, David's always paired with a newbie. The meeting where he is getting a new partner is always goes the same, "You are the best," they say, "you can pass on your knowledge." It makes him feel a like a walking handbook. His retirement is not far away and in some ways, he's looking forward to it but he will miss the thrill of solving a case. "So, what do you think of this case then," John says, interrupting David's thoughts.

"Difficult to say, it does sound a pretty open and shut case but you can never tell. Did I ever tell you about the case of the teacher at school?"

"Yes, you did. You thought the killer was the deputy head as they had a widely known hatred of each other and there was reports of screaming from the deputy head's office and it turned out to be umm oh shit I know this one…"

"It was one of the pupils who'd had enough and thought that

30

it was the only way to improve their school."

"Yes! That's it and how did you discover that?"

"Well no one could place the deputy head outside the school and everything pointed to him being in the school but then it just happened that an ANPR camera caught his car at two minutes after the murder that was over ten miles away from the school so there was no way he could have done it. So it was just a waiting game, I always find that the killer ends up making a mistake at some point and what we did was allow the killer to think we had caught someone and eventually the student, after a number of voluntary interviews to gain statements about the deputy head, suddenly let slip a key bit of information about the murder that only the murderer would know."

"Nice," John says, he bends down and grabs his notepad from the floor of the car and starts to flip through it.

"So, we need to speak to the owner of the Guiseppe's, where they had their date."

"Great! Do you want to take the lead on this one?"

"Are you sure?" John asks. "You okay? You never let me take the lead."

"Yes, I'm okay. I think you are ready and this could be a great case for you to have a go on and anyway, I'll be there the entire time so if you miss anything, I'll pick it up."

"Legend!" John says beaming and for the first time, and possibly the only time that day. David thinks there's a moment of peace as they drive silently in the car while John scribbles down questions.

Chapter 9

Arriving at the restaurant, John knocks on the door and peers in through the window. He sees a woman appear from the kitchen with the blondest hair he's ever seen. She looks seriously pissed off that he has interrupted what was probably her quiet time of the day. As she approaches, she shouts, "Sorry, we aren't open until twelve, I'm afraid. Can you come back a bit later and I'll get a booking in for you?"

John holds up his badge to the glass door. "It's the police we have a couple of questions about a date that happened here last night."

"Oh!" The woman exclaims in shock and starts to unlock the doors, they get stuck on the last lock and she leaves the door open with a firm pull. "I'm so sorry, officers, please come in, come in. I thought you were a customer. You wouldn't believe the amount of people that see a closed sign and just knock anyway."

"That's no worries, this has place has a great reputation! I've heard great things about it. I'm Detective Inspector John Collingham and this is my partner, David."

"Pleased to meet you," David says as he holds out his hand to shake the woman's.

"Pleased to me you, I'm Millie. I'm the owner. Please come this way. She ushers them towards the back of the restaurant. "Thank you, I've only be in charge of the place for about two years, my parents used to own it so I've been updating it a lot.

As she shows them through to the back of the restaurant John can see what she means, there is none of the typical Italian restaurant memorabilia, such as the picture over the Venice canal or the white table clothes with bottles of oil sat on them ready to be never used. He can see that she has put in booths with ornate wooden tables in them and above the kitchen is a neon sign that says Guiseppe's. "I like what you have done with it," John remarks looking around.

"Thank you very much, it's sort of a passion project. I need to do a few more things but eventually it will be just right, please take a seat." David takes the lead as he slides down to the end and John takes a place next to him. "Coffee?" Millie asks.

"If you don't mind, that would be lovely," David says.

"It's no trouble at all, what kind would you like we have every type of coffee going here, it's one of our specialties."

David can see why Guiseppe's is doing so well with Millie at the helm. "A cappuccino would be lovely."

John nods his head. "Same for me please."

As Millie heads off to make the coffees, David looks over at John who has just got his notepad out and is scribbling a few last-minute questions. "All good?" David asks.

"All good, just making sure I've got everything covered."

"That a boy. I'll jump in if I think of anything."

"Thanks mate."

Millie walks back over to them expertly carrying three coffees at once. Something David has always admired whenever he is in a restaurant watching the front of house staff carrying multiple items. Before joining the police, David had tried his hand as a waiter, but after he dropped something pretty much on a nightly basis. It just wasn't his calling. Millie slowly puts down the coffees in front of them and slides over this perfect looking coffee with a flower on top. The strong aroma of coffee hits

David. "Thank you very much," he says, as he goes to take his first sip as Millie sits down.

"So," he says once she's settled in, "we are investigating a murder that happened last night at around 11pm down Barber Alley."

"Oh yes, I saw the news about that this morning on Twitter. Absolutely terrible, I'm so sorry," Millie says.

David and John both stiffen at the news that it had already made it to Twitter, because they hadn't even released a statement so it shouldn't be anywhere at the moment. They have become more accustomed to leaks recently due to social media. It's so easy to ping a post and it suddenly spreads around the town like wildfire. David looks down at John writing notes, he can see he has written LEAK? And circled it twice. Trying not to show that they are shocked by that news, John continues, "Yes, that's the one. We believe that the couple had their first date here and left this restaurant about twenty minutes before the murder happened."

Millie brings her hands to her mouth and her eyes widen in shock as she processes the information.

"So, we just want to ask you a few questions about the couple," David continues.

Taking her hands away from her face, she nods. "Absolutely whatever you need. Ask away."

"So, the couple were here last night, the name it will probably be booked under is Graham."

Millie gets her phone out of her pocket and starts scrolling. She lets out a groan in frustration obviously hitting the wrong button.

"Ah we've only just moved to this new app system and I still can't get my head around it."

34

She is still scrolling when she says, "Ah here we are, Graham, yes they were sat over there by the window. I remember the guy booking it, he sounded nervous."

"It was their first date," David injects.

"Oh, that poor girl, you never expect that to happen and especially round here."

"So, can I ask you did you interact with them at all?"

"I am front of house so I greet everyone as they come in and take their coats and take them to the table, I always think the owner showing people to the table is a nice little touch."

"How did they seem?" David asks.

"He was definitely nervous and was trying to make small talk with his date. I showed them to the table and from where I was stood it looked like it went well. They ordered wine, and then another bottle."

"So, would you say they were intoxicated by the time they left?"

"Do you know what was a bit odd now that I think about it? I don't think he even finished a glass, he was constantly topping hers up."

"Really?" David looks up at her from writing his notes.

"Yeah, normally on first dates both parties either go for it or not but yeah it was definitely her that was drinking more and more."

"Do you know what they were talking about?"

"I don't I'm afraid, it's probably best to talk to Sofia, the waitress who was looking after them that night. She would know what they were talking about and maybe give you more of an insight."

"That would be great, have you got an address or number we could contact her on?"

Millie leans out of the booth and looks back towards the kitchen and says, "She is actually due in about ten/fifteen minutes if you don't mind waiting. I'm sure she would be happy to talk to you, but I don't think there is anything else I could help you with I'm afraid."

David nods "Thank you, Millie. We will wait for Sofia, if that's okay."

"Absolutely. Would you guys like another coffee?"

Picking up his cup and draining the last remnants, he replies, "That would be great, thank you."

As she gathers the cups, John looks up and says, "Can I just ask one question?"

"Sure."

"How did they seem when they left the restaurant?"

"Well I didn't think it went that well, I don't think the mood was that great. The woman was checking her phone constantly. And when they left out the door, they had an awkward hug and went their separate ways"

"Thank you," replies John and David notices as he looks once again at John's notepad, he has written in capital letters THE DATE ENDED BADLY – LEAD – WHAT HAPPENED? Underlined three times.

"Is that all?" Mille asks

"Yes, that's all. Thank you for your time, Millie."

"No worries. I'll get you that coffee," Millie adds and shuffles out of the booth and heads off to the kitchen. John slides out of the booth and gets his phone out.

"I'm going to give HQ a bell, let them know what we have and that we won't be back for a while. I have a feeling that this waitress might just be the witness we need."

David nods, lost in his own thoughts as John puts his phone

to his ear and says hello before making his way down the restaurant. David agrees with John and has a feeling that this whole case might hinge on what happened on this date.

Chapter 10

Back at HQ, Ava puts down the phone. She looks over at Jaimie and says, "The date did not go well at all"

"Really?" says Jamie, looking up from his screen.

"I'm going to head down and tell Jess. How far are you away from finishing that bit of research so I can tell her how it's going?"

"Yeah, not far now, probably about thirty minutes for the preliminary report and then Jess can see it and let us know which one she wants to do in-depth research on. There's definitely some interesting stuff here though. Do you know that the reason his first marriage broke down was due to an extra-marital affair?"

"Great," says Ava, as she stands up and gathers the little note that she had just written.

As she heads down the stairs, she makes her way through the rabbit warren that is this station. When she first worked here, she got lost so many times as everywhere is the same – magnolia with black skirting – it's impossible. She makes her way towards Interview Room One and presses the buzzer. She can hear it go off inside and she can faintly hear the scraping of chairs and Jess saying, "Interview suspended at 11.10." Ava watches as the door handle turns and as Jess pulls the door open, she can see Rupert sat in there. He looks dishevelled and broken. She's never had a chance to interview a suspect, she's always on research duties.

"Ava, you okay?" asks Jess.

"Yes, I just wanted to let you know that John has just called from the restaurant. The date ended badly apparently. They weren't speaking and she was on her phone when she left and they had an awkward hug but yeah, it didn't seem it went well at all. David and John are just waiting for the waitress that waited on them last night so they can find out what exactly went wrong. They think they will have info in about forty-five minutes but John wanted to let you know."

"That's great thank you, he's not giving us anything so at least this might frighten him into saying something."

She pauses. Ava can see she's thinking about what the possible outcomes could be. Then looking back up at Ava, "How's the research going?"

"Yeah good, we are getting there I reckon in the next half an hour we will have a good overview of all his socials, dating app history, messages and total background. Jamie has said to let us know which direction you want us to go in. He seems pretty excited by his findings. He was thrilled to tell me that Rupert's divorce was because of an affair."

Jess's ears suddenly prick as though she hasn't been listening to Ava but that last bit of information has piqued her interest.

"What? It ended because of an affair?"

"Yeah, apparently so"

"He's been really cagey about it and won't say anything and his lawyer won't let us talk about it. I might try and raise it if he has a problem with keeping it in his pants, it might lead us to somewhere. Can you bring that info straight down when you have it? Don't worry about interrupting, we need to get something soon otherwise we can't hold him any longer."

"Yes, no problem, will do. Oh, and one more thing, John says it's been leaked on Twitter already," Ava says.

"Oh, for fuck sake! Can you do me a favour and when you finished with report find the account and see if we can locate this individual? We need to get a hold of these leaks!"

Ava nods and turns. She races upstairs to tell Jaimie he needs to get that report printed as soon as.

Chapter 11

Jess returns to the interview feeling invigorated. She finally knows she has something to push him on – the bad date. The last hour of question has just been going over the same the stuff and almost verbatim answers, but now thanks to Ava she has a different line to go on. She can't guess how this case is going to go, she normally gets a sense if the person is innocent or guilty but Rupert is giving none of these signs. It makes her think he's hiding something. She now feels the pressure to get this case wrapped up before the press phone calls begin. She was hoping to keep it under the radar until they had some solid evidence to charge Rupert on. She's going to leave the affair regarding the divorce in her back pocket as she feels it will come in useful later. "So, Rupert can I ask how did the date ended and what did you do after you left the restaurant?" She notices Rupert stiffen slightly.

"It ended really well, we were arranging a second date before we even left the restaurant, she was checking her calendar on her phone for a suitable evening next week. We laughed and joked and I didn't know how to end it so I gave her a hug. I didn't think it was appropriate to go in for a kiss on for the first date. And then I walked back along Everyman Street, you know just off the High Street walking back towards the edge of town and that's when I heard that terrible scream from Barber Alley where I had cut through earlier that evening and when I arrived there was the body lying there and then it all went black when I spotted the beanie that Jennifer had put on at the end of the date."

"Okay, Rupert, I'm going to level with you, I don't think any of that is true, is it? We are currently speaking to the restaurant where you ate last night and a witness there seems to think that the date did not end well and we have another witness who was there last night, so just please be truthful with us. It will only help you in the end."

"I'm telling the truth!" Rupert says in almost desperate tone. "Why on earth would I lie? My entire career and life is on the line if I don't tell the truth."

"So, what happened on the date then?"

Rupert looks down at his hands and then back up at Jess, she can sense he has something to tell her that he doesn't want to.

Chapter 12

This is going better than I could have ever expected. Rupert's been in custody for over twelve hours. The image of him getting arrested is still in my mind and the pure glee I felt. I still can't believe it worked. Let's just hope the next few hours goes the way I planned.

I know the police have been sent out to the restaurant. I've been watching them all carefully I am literally giddy with excitement when they discover what I have in store for them there. I thought they would have held a press conference by now and then I can carry on with the next phase of my plan. I sort of hope the little tweet I sent out pushes them into it and also creates a bit of a frenzy in town.

It's so frustrating I just want him locked up for what he has done. This was the only way that I could think of. I had so many scenarios that I had thought of but in the end, it wasn't a difficult decision. Murder is the one crime that carries the longest sentence, so it just made sense.

I guess all I can do now is to sit and wait and hopefully watch Rupert hang himself in all the evidence. I just want this done and dusted!

Chapter 13

Sofia is rushing out of the front door; she had hoped to get the flat tidied this morning but she convinced herself that it was better to do it later when she gets back in after work but even she knows this isn't going to happen. She didn't sleep well last night, she kept tossing and turning and her thoughts kept returning to the tweet she saw when she got in from work. Barber Alley was just down from the restaurant she works at and the description sound awfully like the couple she had been waiting on last night. She really hopes she's wrong.

Doing the awkward half running half walking thing, Sofia rushes up the hill. Millie hates anyone being late and she's the first one in for today's shift to help get the restaurant ready. As she approaches the restaurant and pushes the door open, she is startled to see two men who appear to be waiting for her, judging by the fact that they both looked up eagerly when she walked in. She had been prepared for this; they must be the police.

The younger one slides out of the bench and approaches her. "Hello, are you Sofia?"

"Yes," she replies.

"Brilliant, I'm David, I'm a detective and we are working on a murder that happened down at Barber Alley."

"Yes, I saw that on Twitter last night, I can't believe it," she says, she fails to tell the officers what else she had seen on Twitter. She considers saying something but thinks better of it. She can't do anything about it now.

"Do you mind if we ask you some questions?"

"Sure, no problem. As long as is it okay with Millie, my boss."

"It's fine we've already spoken to Millie and she suggested you might be able to give us more of an insight into what happened at the meal, so if we can get you in this booth..." David says as he gestures toward the table they were sat in when she arrived.

The other officer stands up when they get near and introduces himself and holds out his hand, "Hello I'm Detective Inspector John Collingham, thank you for taking some time to speak to us."

She returns the handshake. "No problem, I'm just happy to help you."

They all sit down and David gets his notepad out and holds his pen ready to write. "So, can you tell us what happened during the meal?"

"Yes. Millie showed them to the seat and then I took their orders. They both seemed pretty nervous, I overheard them saying that this was their first date in a while. So, I assumed that was why they were nervous. They ordered the starter and when I went back over, I could hear they were talking about their jobs. It sounded like he worked in TV or film or something along that line, he was saying what programs he had worked on and asking if she had heard any of them."

"How was the mood then? Did there seem to be any tension? Any looks to you to indicate there was a problem?"

"No, I didn't think there was a problem at all, I thought it all seemed pretty normal," Sofia says.

"Were they drinking a lot?" John chips in.

"She was drinking, he seemed to be nursing his wine, I just

thought maybe he didn't want to lose control or embarrass himself. People deal with dates differently she clearly needed a bit of Dutch courage which he was helping with by topping up her glass every time it went slightly low."

John also with his notepad out, writes something down she can't see it, but she sees David's eye look across and then scribble something on his pad. "Please Sofia carry on, what happened next?"

"So, after I took the order for the main, the mood seemed fine and he excused himself and asked me where the toilet was. While he was away from the table, she was clearly texting mates and I think he had gone to call someone in the bathroom. You've both seen First Dates, right? It's what happens on these Tinder dates." David nods and John is still writing. "So, when he came back, I gave them about ten minutes and when I took the mains over the mood was definitely different, they were speaking in very angry whispers and they stopped as I got closer. she wasn't smiling or talking, and he looked worried and a bit sorry for himself. I kept up a smiley attitude as I gave them their mains explaining what each one was and as I was walking away, I did hear something now that I think about it."

David looks up, this is the moment she thinks this is what they want to hear and what she had been worrying about all night.

"What did you hear?"

Taking a deep breath, "I heard the woman say 'You can't just go around doing that to women, it's not right.' Or something like that."

David and John look at each other. John immediately gets up and calls HQ.

Chapter 14

Jess is stood outside the interview room with Andrew, they have just decided to take a ten-minute hiatus on the advice of Rupert's lawyer. She is feeling highly frustrated because she literally thought that they were about to break him and get something out of him when the lawyer stepped in and said that they needed a break as they and been interviewing his client for over two hours and he would like ten minutes to talk to him.

Andrew turned to Jess. "There's no point of waiting out here like sitting ducks. Come on, let's get a coffee from the machine down the hall."

Jess weighs it up and eventually relents, nodding slowly. "What's going on, sugar?" Andrews asks.

Andrew had taken to calling her a number of nicknames over the years. It ranged from rock star to bud and now onto sugar. He often calls Jess his work wife and Jess is so glad that they have such a close working relationship as he always looks out for her and more importantly always has a different perspective on cases which is helpful. They are the epitome of yin and yang. "Nothing, it's just I'm frustrated because he is coming across as not guilty but he was there at the crime scene, bent over the body. He isn't giving anything away and the clock is ticking before we have to release him."

As they walk into the kitchen, she kicks the plastic bin in frustration and shouts, "Fuck!"

"Whoa! Don't take it out on the bin! Just hang in there. We

will get something which means we can charge him. All we need is a tiny bit of evidence or witness statement to nail him to the scene. I know that the fact the date did not go well is not strong enough to charge him but if we pull at that thread, he may give away something else."

"I know, I just thought if I let him know that we knew the date didn't end as well as he said it did, he might have got a bit thrown, but that lawyer keeps jumping in giving him time to think. There's something off about having your ex-brother-in-law as your lawyer, blurring boundaries don't you think?" Jess replies.

"Each to their own, you can have your mum represent you if you so wish. It's just part of the system," Andrew says, grabbing some cups from the cupboard. She loves to excel at things, she has always been good at everything she had put her mind to. She had been single mum and managed to keep her promotion and had solved some of the force's biggest cases in this time, some even in record time. That's what the big bosses like about her, she gets results. This is why she is getting so frustrated, she never fails to almost get it solved in the first interview but she is starting to think and possibly worry that this isn't going to be so easy.

"Anyway," Andrew carries on, "we've got Team C who we haven't heard back from yet at the crime scene and forensic detail, as soon as they get something we can they charge the bastard. Tea or coffee?"

"Yeah, I suppose you are right. Coffee, please."

"Great, one coffee coming right up, so let's talk about something else. Case talk doesn't need to be everything we talk about, how's your love life going you been on any dates yet?"

"No not recently, when do I have the time?"

"Whenever you are off, why are you not looking for

someone it's been a long time now?" Andrew jokes with her.

"Not you as well, I already have my mum going on about my love life at home, I don't need it at work too."

"Ooh someone is touchy today. I just want you to be happy sugar."

Annoyed as she was, he was right it had been a good while since she dated anybody let alone slept with anyone. The last man she had slept with was Joseph's dad who she had met a few years ago and when a few solid dates and few very fun nights had ended in a pregnancy. She had decided to keep the baby and do the single mum life. Everybody around her had always asked why didn't she stay with Joseph's dad, she had started to fall for him but when she told him about the pregnancy it was clear there was no love there from him it was pure lust and after talking it through, they had both decided that it would never work and it was just sex. She has been hurt by the whole ordeal but she didn't want to be with someone just for a baby. He promised that he was going to be involved every step of the way and that he was always going to be around for Joseph, all of which lasted the first two months of Joseph being born when he came to her and explained that he had met someone a few months back and that he was moving up to Newcastle to be with her. He said that he would obviously help with the money. Jess told him to fuck off and that she didn't need the money and that money can't replace not being there for his son. They argued and argued and Jess considered getting lawyers involved but, in the end, he just upped and left one night and changed his phone number. She knows because she keeps tabs on him from the police database, she has figured out that the relationship probably didn't work because he was now living over in Liverpool, but even despite this set back with Joseph's dad she put her mind to it made sure he wanted for nothing and never wanted him to feel like he didn't have a dad. That meant she put her own needs at the back of her mind and all she focused on was Joseph.

"Do you know, I think I might have the perfect person for you?" Andrew says. "How would feel if I set you up on a blind date?"

"I would rather spend a night in the cells with all the people I've locked up," she says laughing out loud.

"Ah come on, just be open to it! I'm not actually going to give you a choice, let me set it up and please do it for me? Plus, if you two hit it off it means that we can then go on double dates and there's no awkwardness because I would already love the guy, I wouldn't feel the need to be protective over you." Taking a sip of her coffee, "Fine, do what you must."

"Shall we go back in? They have had plenty of time now?" Andrew says.

As they are walking back to the interview room. Ava appears again with a printout for them, it's the background report that she promised. As Jess looks through, she sees Rupert's Tinder history. There is a list of every girl that Rupert has swiped right on, he definitely has a type. She can see that he has been working in TV since he was twenty-one. Some programs she had heard about others she hadn't and she can see in black and white that the reason for the divorce from his first wife was extra marital relations. The next page is details of messages and emails he has sent in the last twenty-four hours. She would look at them in a bit more detail when she goes back into the room. Ava is still stood there when she comes to the end of her brief look at the report. "This is great, thank you. Can you and Jamie just dig a bit more into his divorce and can we start looking at his phone locations? We need to place him there at the scene. Is there anything else Ava?"

"Yes, John has been on the phone again. They have finally spoken to the waitress and they have found something interesting."

Chapter 15

Rupert's head is buzzing, he has just been speaking to Jason for ten minutes about what he should and shouldn't answer, but he can't for the life of him remember what has just been said. He just wants this over with. He trusts Jason so much they have been friends for years and it was Jason who he met his first wife through. They had been childhood friends when he went around to Jason's house for dinner one night and that's when he saw her for the first time, the most beautiful girl he had ever seen. He was immediately smitten and started to chat to her separately and eventually he wanted to ask her out. He checked with Jason because he didn't want to ruin their friendship. When Jason said he was all for it and he couldn't be happier for both of them if it worked. He has never told Jason the real reason why the divorce came about as he didn't want to cause trouble between all of them.

"Are you all good?" Jason asks.

"All good. I just want this to be over, when can they let me go?"

"Well, they are running out of time to be honest, mate, but just answer all the questions honestly and try to answer them in the way we discussed and we will be having you out of here in no time."

"Thanks, mate. I don't what I would do without you, you sure it's not odd all this for you?"

"Of course, not mate, it's just unfortunate set of events that's all, you would do the same for me if the shoe was on the other foot. Now are there any other ques…"

Jason is interrupted as the door opens, he sees Jess and Andrew walk back in both carrying cups. In her other hand Jess is holding a ream of paper stapled together. He reckons that's all about him and he thinks he notices a moment of glee across Jess's face. He has a sinking feeling in the pit of his stomach. "Sorry, we really need to continue this interview and you have had ten minutes with your client."

Jason nods slowly and they start to take a seat, Rupert's tired brain is trying to remember how Jason told him to answer the questions.

"So…" Jess says as she hits the record button, "We are continuing with the interview of Rupert Graham at," she checks her watch, "13:30. So Rupert, I asked you earlier what happened between main and dessert?"

Rupert's brain is absolutely screaming, "Nothing happened." He says,

"Come on Rupert, you must have realised by now that we have spoken to someone at the restaurant, everybody in this room probably knows what happened so why don't you do us all a favour and just tell us what exactly happened between you and Jennifer last night at Guiseppe's?"

"Nothing happened," he repeats feeling trapped in a corner, he has so many thoughts he can't think straight, they will never understand as soon as he says it, he will look guilty and he knows it. It was just an innocent mistake. Jess looks at Andrew in exasperation. Andrew then looks straight at Rupert as though he is trying to read his thoughts. "Okay," he says after what seems like ages, "I think what's happened here is simple I think that you went to this restaurant you were having a great time thinking that this date was leading somewhere and you wanted to keep a clear head and get her a little tipsy hence why you went through about two bottles of wine but yet you seemed to nurse one glass all night. This all went wrong for you when she rejected you just after mains, she told you that she wasn't having a good time, and I believe that this was the turning point in the evening, but you thought you would give it another go maybe dessert would turn it around."

"No, that didn't happen."

"Don't worry, mate, I've seen it lots of times. Now I believe you both left without talking, you tried to hug her and then she reiterated that it was never going to happen. That's when that switch flicked and a plan appeared like magic for you."

"No, that didn't happen," Rupert said trying not to show his frustration at these lies swirling around the room.

"Now I believe you didn't know what happened next. The red mist, as they say, descended and the next thing you know you are over her body and Jennifer Green is dead! Tell me If I am wrong."

"You are wrong!" Rupert says looking straight at Andrew.

"What happened then? Tell me Rupert." He slams his fists down on the table. "You are the only one who can help yourself here and you are wasting our time."

"I didn't mean to touch her," Rupert shouts into the room before he has time to think. Jess stops writing her notes. Rupert puts his head in hands, trying to think.

Andrew and Jess lean forward slightly. "What do you mean you didn't mean to touch her?" Jess says tentatively

He's going to have to say it, he just hopes they believe him "I didn't kill her! But there was an incident between main and dessert, but I want it on record that it was resolved before we even ordered dessert. I thought the date was going well so I put my hand on her leg and squeezed it. It's been so long since I've been on a date and lots of people had been giving me advice and I just made a mistake! She quickly told me off and said you shouldn't do that to women. I said I was sorry and explained what had happened and how it had been so long since I had been on date and she accepted my apology and we ended the date on good terms, I assure you. I was nowhere near Barber Alley as I have explained I was walking on Everyman Street when I heard a scream. I had just text Jason to say how well the date went."

Jess looks over at Jason, who nods. "That's true he texted me saying how well he thought it went."

Rupert puts his head in his hands and begins to breath rapidly. "I didn't kill her. I didn't fucking kill her." The image of the beanie is flashing up in his mind and the blue lights and then a white light appears in front of the blue lights and all he can hear is himself saying over and over and over again. "I didn't kill her." His brain is firing thoughts at him, like a machine gun. There's no way out of this! He can't hear himself anymore, it's just white noise. The only words he hears faintly in the distance is the voice of Jess shouting, "Can we get a medic in here please?"

Chapter 16

Olivia and Isabella, Team C, are at the scene with CSI as they are dusting for fingerprints and taking samples. They are both relatively new to the department. Olivia had just come on a transfer from London because her fiancé had just got a job just outside Winchester. She had stayed in London until a suitable position came up and then moved as soon as she could. She had been paired with Isabella as soon as she arrived, and they got on like a house on fire. They both liked the same stuff and they very occasionally disagreed on anything and loved to spend time together outside the office. They had been to the pub that previous evening not that far down the road from where Rupert and Jennifer were having their date. So strange, she thought, as they discussed it on the way to the job, how two minutes down the road they were laughing and joking while someone was getting murdered. She is watching the chief CSI officer taking photos and slowly moving around the crime scene where the white tape outlining where the body of Jennifer Green lay just over fifteen hours ago. She thinks his name is Dave but to be honest she wasn't listening. She's still nursing a hangover from last night and she was so relieved when Jess had said they were on crime scene because it's a lot of standing around. The one bit she isn't looking forward to is the autopsy.

Isabella comes over with two coffees. "Cappuccino with a double shot in it, that should help blow away the cobwebs from last night," she says handing over one that says Olive on the side.

"Thanks very much," she says as she takes a sip. "How are you feeling after last night?"

"Not bad, but I never really get hangovers anyway and I didn't mix my drinks."

"I didn't want to, but I think I got carried away. It was such a fun night!"

"It's always fun!" Isabella says, smiling.

"Well, I suppose we should go and see how they are getting on," Olivia said putting in an enormous amount of effort to get up from the wall she had been leaning against.

As she wanders over, Dave stops doing what he is doing. "How's it going? Have you found any evidence?"

"We've found a footprint which we are just taking a sample of, for you to take back and compare to the suspect's footwear, although you know this is one of the busiest cut throughs in town. Let's just hope we can find something else solid. The only thing in our favour is that it was a cold frosty night so everything is preserved a little better."

"Amazing, thank you. What's the chances of finding something?" Isabella adds.

"Hopefully there's a bit of skin or sweat from the attacker that's on the ground somewhere. It's just going to be a long wait I'm afraid, until we have 100% covered the area"

"Thanks, we are just going to go and wait in the café if you need us for anything," Olivia says and with that they both turn and head towards to the coffee shop which has a window facing Barber Alley. Even not being a specialist in this area she knows that without solid evidence the case can't gain traction to charge the guy as he could have just stumbled across the scene.

"Do you want to give HQ a call and let them know that a footprint will be coming their way and when do they want us to head to the autopsy?" Olivia says to Isabella. "I would do it but I think I need another coffee before my brain can even function. Do you want another?"

"Yeah, flat white for me please."

Olivia nods and gets up and goes towards the counter as Isabella starts dialling the number for HQ and she just is just out earshot when she gets through.

"Hello, what can I get for you?" the barista says with that got up at six smile. Olivia hates early risers and especially happy ones, she thinks the bed is the best place to be and designed to be stayed in for as long as you can.

"Cappuccino with double shot and a flat white please, under the name Olivia."

"Coming right up," again with another cheery smile. As the cup goes under the machine and the familiar sound of the coffee beans being ground, the barista chips in, "So what happened over there then?"

"I'm sorry that's police business, I can't really say," Olivia says.

"Oh really! Well, if I can help in any way I'm happy to."

"Brilliant thank you," she says hoping that is the end of the conversation.

"Because we have a brilliant CCTV system here."

Not even listening anymore because she just wants the coffee and wants this conversation to end, she gets her phone out to start mindlessly scrolling, "Great well if we need to, we'll be in touch."

Still smiling "Well anything I can do to help, my dad used to be a policeman and I'm always ready to help out." He places the coffee on the counter and as she goes to pay, he puts his hand out. "No need to pay, least I can do."

She puts her card away and thinks the least she can probably do is give the guy a smile and say thank you. She really needs to get rid of this hangover. She heads back over to Isabella who is just ending the call and slumps back down into the metal chair next to her and puts the coffees on the table, she notices they have put her name as Oliver.

"No, that did not happen. Oh my god is everyone okay?" Isabella is asking on the phone. Olivia looks over to her and waves her hand which Isabella notices and holds up two fingers to indicate two minutes and mouths, you'll never guess what's happened.

Olivia nods, intrigued about what she is about to hear and takes a sip of her coffee, she is so grateful that the coffee shop was near. She needs to stop going so hard on these night outs. She thought it was only going to be a few drinks and then end of the night but once her and Isabella start it can turn from finishing at ten to finishing at two. Isabella is twenty-five and is full of beans and enthusiasm and can just get out of bed after a heavy night with no problems. Olivia's just turned thirty-one and she seems to have lost the ability to do that, with every drink she has it seems to add about two hours to her hangover! She didn't have a problem with turning thirty as everyone from her boyfriend to her mum told her she would, they all thought she would freak out and have that turning thirty blip, but she's loved it so far, she had it more when she turned twenty-nine than thirty. The hangover thing is really the only thing that has changed. She hears Isabella say good bye on the phone and hang up.

"You will never guess what's happened?"

"What?" Olivia says and she takes another sip of her coffee.

"So that was Ava, and she said it is all going off at the station. Basically, she said," she pauses to make sure no one is around and that the barista is far enough away and says in a hush whisper, "They have found evidence of the date not going well according the witnesses and that his divorce was because of extra marital affair that shows he's potentially a sex pest, but the mad thing is that apparently during the interview, Jess and Andrew were really drilling down hard on him and the guy only went and had a full blown panic attack."

"No way," Olivia says louder than she meant to and looks around to make sure that the no one heard her. "How the fuck did they let that happen?"

"No idea, but Ava said that the whole station went off and there were people running everywhere scrambling the doctor and all sorts of panic. They thought he was having a heart attack to start with apparently. Jess is furious!"

"Yeah, I bet she is, they've just fucked up their chance of ever getting a solid confession out of him. It's just going to have to be evidence alone. Witness statements are all well and good but they can easily be picked apart in court."

"This means that we really need something from here or the autopsy, doesn't it?"

Sighing out loud. "Yes, it does, just when I thought we were in for a slightly easier day. We need to get that footprint back soon as and hopefully there is some skin or some sort of DNA here to get this bastard. Right, shall we get back out there and hurry these boys along?"

"Sounds good to me," Isabella says as she grabs her coffee off the table. Too busy thinking about the evidence and what they need to do next, she forgets all about the CCTV that was mentioned by the barista as she waves to him from the door shouting a thank you. She just hopes this hangover is going to pass because she needs to be on her A game.

Chapter 17

Coming around in the police doctor's office was a shock! Rupert had no idea what had happened but as he looked over in the corner, Jason was sat there with a worried look on his face and Jess and Andrew were nowhere to be seen. "What happened?" he asks Jason.

Looking up, shocked to see him awake, Jason says, "Mate, you had a full-blown panic attack. I thought you were dead for a minute. They kept pushing you with questions about the date and you admitted you touched her under the table. What were you thinking? You've landed yourself right in the shit here you know that right."

It all comes flooding back to him shouting that he didn't mean to touch her and then it all went black.

"Yes, I know that. It was a misjudged move, I thought we were getting on and thought it was the right thing to do and immediately regretted it. You told me to be flirty and fun!"

Standing up now, looking infuriated. "I told you to be fun and flirty, not a downright fucking creepy old man. You've fucked this right up."

He runs his hands through his hair in despair. "You know they are going to try to throw the book at you now? What were you thinking, why were you even there you had left the date why did you turn around?"

"Wouldn't you do the same, if you heard a blood curdling scream?"

He stops and walks closer to Rupert. "Not if it meant that I was going to be done for fucking murder!"

"I didn't do it!" Rupert says, sounding frustrated.

"I do believe you, Rupert. I do." Even Rupert can see that there is doubt behind his eyes. "But even someone as clever as you can see that this does not look good and these people, they don't care about you or how this affects you, they want a result and they don't really care about how they get it, the evidence is just piling up against you mate! You get that right?"

"What am I going to do Jase?" he pleads.

Trying to sound calmer, he says, "Well the good thing is that because they caused you to have a panic attack, they are no longer allowed near you, which is good for us. This mean they need physical evidence before they can interview you again and the clock is ticking towards the time, they either have to charge you or let you go pending investigation, but believe me that doesn't mean you are free and easy. Anything they get they can come and arrest you." Feeling sick he just can't believe this is happening.

"So how long until I can go home?" he asks out of desperation, he just wants to be home. He has never wanted his flat more than he does right now.

"Soon, hopefully soon, we are just waiting for them to come down from their bitch fit and then they can hold you right up to the time which according to my watch." he shuffles his watch out from his wrist, "umm… about … four hours to go. But I know that they are working at the scene and are trying to desperately find any evidence they can, so for now we can just sit tight. If you just say when the doctor comes back in a minute that you still aren't feeling too well hopefully, we can keep you in here with me until they can let you go." Rupert nods. Jason comes over and places his hand on his shoulder. "This will all be resolved I promise."

Rupert starts to almost well up before catching himself, he is so pleased that Jason has his back, at that moment the doctor comes back in.

"Ah you're awake!" he says with a smile. Rupert thinks how can you be that happy when you are dealing with criminals all day everyday but this guy seems to be managing it. "How are you feeling, Mr Graham, you gave us all quite a shock there?"

"Not too well doc I'm afraid I still feel really light headed," he says hoping that the doctor is going to leave him in here.

The doctor looks at him and says, "You do still look a bit worse for wear, I think it is probably for the best to leave you in here for the time being."

"Thank you," Rupert says.

As the doctor leaves the room. There is silence as both men are deep in thought. Rupert is praying that there is a way out of this.

Chapter 18

The air in Jess's office is fraught, not because while Rupert and Jason were coming to terms with the situation that just happened. Once Rupert was removed from the interview room. She gave Andrew a look that could kill. She loves him to pieces but he has just pushed their only suspect to the point of a panic attack. She knows he was just doing it to help her but they have literally just blown their chance to get a confession as his prick of a lawyer had great delight in telling them that they were not allowed near his client at this time due to the amount of pressure that had just been witnessed in the interview. As she went up to her office and slammed her door, she got a phone call that was an even bigger blow, the superintendent has been informed of the incident, that's the problem with police stations, fire's spread slower than information does! They agreed that the suspect cannot be interviewed while he is in that state and that they have been advised to stay away from him. It means the odds of charging him in the next four hours have dramatically shrunk and she knows it and the team knows it. All they can do now is keep searching for evidence to put him at the scene at the time of the killing or if they have enough witnesses and statements that could be enough to evoke a charge but with only the waitress and the owner, she knows they would be taken apart in seconds in a court room.

After the phone call she just sat there in silence, replaying the whole interview in her head getting more and more frustrated and she looks up she can see the board outside that she had written on earlier that day. She knew it was going to be a complicated case but she thought she would be able to get a confession and it would be another win for her department, another bad guy off the street.

She's looking directly at the picture of Jennifer Green that's been pinned underneath her name and she can't help but notice her eyes were so beautiful and so innocent at the same time and suddenly the frustration becomes too much for Jess as she picks up her stapler and launches it across the room. "Fuck!". She notices her team looking at her through the glass office that she now wished was just solid walls.

Andrew approaches, both of them know that this conversation is not going to go well but both also know they need to have it if they are going to carry on.

That's how their relationship has always worked. As he knocks on the door. She shouts, "Come in." As he enters, he already looks sheepish. "Look Jess I'm sorry about that, I just knew you were feeling frustrated and I thought I could just go heavy and break the man."

"You thought I was feeling frustrated! How fucking dare you," she said in a stern but low volume tone, "I was frustrated for the case and the fact that a woman died last night and we turn up to find the same man she had a date that finished no more than ten minutes before she was murdered standing of the body, this should have been." She corrects herself it's not over yet. "Should be, an open and fucking shut case, we were getting there, there was no need for you to ride in on your big high horse and try to save the day. I know you like to think you're helping Andrew, but what you just did there has not only right royally fucked us, but you fucked me too!"

"I know, Jess, I'm so sorry I thought it was the best tactic how was I meant to know the man was going to have a panic attack! That has never happened to me in all my years on the force and I have interviewed some of the most dangerous criminals this country has ever seen."

She knows that, she knows that this is small fry for Andrew and that is why she generally enjoys having him around.

"I know, I know, Andrew, and I don't want to sound ungrateful but I don't need rescuing in those scenarios. I need us to work together and not go hell for leather! I know I was frustrated but we can't even go near the guy! That lawyer is just going to wait this out until they can leave and then that's it, we have to have solid evidence or enough witness statements to fill an entire court room."

"I'm sorry Jess, I've really let you down. I was just trying to help!" He says as he slumps down in the chair opposite her. "What are we going to do now?"

"We need to hope that there is some fucking happy God up there to provide use with some ironclad evidence."

"Okay, I'll put some pressure on the teams to get them working even harder, is there anything you want done?"

"Yes, I want Team A back here immediately and trawling through CCTV, from the High Street and surrounding areas. Get them to check in with Team C on scene and see if they can see any obvious camera points, we need to check."

"Will do, boss." He starts to get up.

"Oh, and another thing, Andrew," He pauses as he opens the door "Don't ever fucking do that again, I love you to pieces but if you cause another suspect to have any sort of episode, then I'm afraid it will only be social time for us." She doesn't mean to sound so cruel but the door is open and she doesn't want everyone thinking that he has gotten away with it. She hopes he understands. "Yes of course, Jess," he says giving her a knowing look that they are okay.

She gets up and goes out in to the main office. "Guys can I have your attention?" Ava and Jamie stop what they are doing and a few other officers from other teams and the ground force who are milling about also stop what they are doing. "So, as you are aware there was an incident earlier in the interview and the official line to any press is that the suspect had a funny turn and that is why we have not made any moves yet on a charge, as the wolves are already at the door, so do expect your phones to start ringing soon. Ava and Jamie, make sure the others know!"

With that she turns back and head back to her office and shuts the door. She needs to think.

Chapter 19

John and David are just leaving the restaurant when they get the call from HQ. John picks up the phone and starts to walk up the street away from David.

David has started to notice that John never likes to talk on the phone near anyone, he always walks away, he thinks its years of people accidently hearing him. David starts to wander down the road. Still thinking about the waitress and the fear in her eyes when she retold the story and asked at the end before they left, she grabbed David's arm and said, "You will charge him right? People like that need locking up. I'll help in anyway if you need an official statement, I'm happy to come down to the station." David was struck for a moment about why she was so insistent but just chalked it up to the fact that she was scared.

He wanders down the road for about a minute and then suddenly realises he is walking in the footsteps of Jennifer as he approaches the cut through known as Barber Alley, he can see the CSI tent at the end blocking his way through. He decides to go and see what the girls are up to. He's sure John will be down soon after his phone call. He carries on past the entrance to Barber Alley and to the street just down from it and posts Olivia and Isabella down there chatting and drinking coffee. He has really enjoyed getting to know them since they arrived. He was always considered the youngest in the team and now that they are here, he feels that the team is more evenly balanced.

He really fancied Isabella when she first arrived and they got on like a house on fire. She asked him for a drink and he was thrilled and was thinking that it was a potential date but that all came crashing down when she walked in with her boyfriend. It was an awkward evening for the three of them. With David trying to act happy but actually dying of embarrassment. He still fancies her but he knows there is nothing he can do about it, and he really likes the social side that Olivia and Isabella have brought since they arrived at the station.

"You all right?" he calls out to them.

"You all right, Big Dave?" Olivia shouts out, she's started calling him Big Dave since another Dave joined the team. Isabella and Olivia decided on their own that they needed a way to distinguish between them so he was now known as Big Dave, he hated it at the beginning but now he's just grown used to it. "What you doing down here? Thought you were interviewing the witnesses at the restaurant."

"Oh, we have just finished with the waitress and John has taken a phone call so I started walking down the hill and saw the alleyway. How have you two been getting on?"

"Not bad, just waiting for CSI to finish up before we go to the autopsy, because they are extracting a footprint for us to take back to the office. Have you heard about what happened at the station?"

"No, not heard anything."

"The suspect had a full-on panic attack in the interview."

"No fucking way! That screams guilty as sin."

Playfully hitting Isabella, Olivia says, "Yes that's what I said, guilty as sin, she said it sounds like not guilty."

"Do you really think that, Izzy?" he says.

"I don't know it just all seems a bit to convenient," Isabella says, her breath steaming after sipping her coffee.

69

"Hmmm I'm not so sure, that waitress seemed pretty shaken up and she seemed pretty scared."

"Someone got a thing for the waitress, have they?" Teases Olivia.

"No," David protests, sounding a bit like a petulant child, more embarrassed than annoyed. "Nothing like that."

"Yeah, yeah!" Isabella joins in.

"Shut up, you dick!" He says with a smile on his face.

"Who's a dick?" John says startling everyone with his sudden presence.

"Jesus, John, why do you always sneak up on people?" Olivia says.

"Because that way Olivia, you can always hear what other people say about you," he says, with a big grin on his face. John never uses a nickname.

"We were just discussing what happened at the station," David says, keeping his voice low to make sure no one outside the four of them could hear.

"Ah yes, that's what I was coming to talk to you about. I've just spoken to HQ and they want us to scope the area for every CCTV point. That includes you two," John says indicating at Olivia and Isabella, who immediately look annoyed and as though they are about to say something. They look at each other as though they are having conversation and then look back at John.

"Sure, no problem," says Isabella

"Great," John says ignoring what he just saw. "Can you two start looking at the route from the restaurant to the alley and we will have a look at all the entrance points to Barber Alley?"

Finishing her coffee, Oliva says, "No problem, come on Izzy. See you later guys. I'll drop you a text Big Dave, with the locations of each CCTV for you guys at the office. If you see Jess say we have a footprint and we are going to head to the autopsy as soon as we have it."

"Will do," says David.

As they watch their colleagues leave, chatting away as they go. John gets his phone out and starts checking the map. "So, if you canvas this road and that road there," he says as he points to the map. "I'll take these two."

"Great, want to meet back here in like twenty minutes?" David says just looking at the phone.

"Sounds good to me," John replies and starts turning to walk down the street. As they part ways they both have their back to the coffee shop where Isabella and Olivia have just been and they both completely miss the CCTV camera attached underneath the roof.

Chapter 20

Rupert and Jason are still in the doctor's room at the police station, they have been here for what seems like a lifetime but in reality, and Rupert knows this because Jason keeps doing a time check every thirty minutes, they have been waiting for three and half hours. Every time the next half an hour goes by, Jason sounds a little bit more relaxed. Rupert knows that once it goes past four hours, they can't hold him anymore. He wasn't really paying attention before the last time check; he was away with his thoughts thinking about what to do next and what happens if this doesn't go the way Jason is thinking and they charge him. He will have to tell his mum and work will have to be informed he could literally lose everything, all because he stupidly touched a girl he was on a date with, which makes him look as guilty as sin. He also knows that passing out in an interview with a panic attack has not done him any favours here. He keeps trying to talk about it with Jason but all Jason wants to do is run out the clock so they can get out of here and regroup and reassess. Jason has wanted to be a lawyer for as long as Rupert has known him. Right from teenagers Jason has been obsessed with law and getting justice and when Rupert went off to unit and did media studies, when he was making films and messing out about the unit's TV studio, Jason had his head in a book and worked really hard. Jason's never been a going out sort of guy, he's very level headed and is always reliable, and that's why he is so good at what he does and is considered one of the best lawyers in the area. Rupert is so glad he is here.

"Right here we go," Jason gleefully announces. "We've got ten minutes and then I reckon they will make us wait for about ten more before they come and tell us you are free to go."

"Thank god," Rupert sighs. "I think that doctor is getting a little bit sick of us taking up his room."

"That's the law, mate, if they want a lawsuit on their hands, they can put you back in a cell but I would take great joy in taking on that case, it would be open and shut by the time they put the key in the lock."

They sit in silence for the next ten minutes. Rupert watching the clock, counting and wishing it would just move faster. He's allowing himself to imagine getting back to his flat that he used to share with his ex-wife and thinking that he might order himself a takeaway and try to get back to some sort of normality and put these last twenty-four hours behind him. The little voice in the back of his head is reminding him that it's not over yet. The news they might come through with, is that they are charging him and then he won't set foot back in the flat for a long time and even if they do let him go it's far from over, he is still a suspect in a murder case. He thinks that it seems so easy on the TV dramas and documentaries that when someone is not responsible it takes a bit of time but it all comes right in the end. He knows that's not what life is like and as Jason keeps saying all they want to do is put a name to this murder and right now his is the only name they have.

"Time!" Jason shouts. "Right I'm going to go and find them and demand they let us leave right now, I think they would have charged you by now to be honest." He buzzes the door to be let out and the doctor looking a bit shocked that someone has buzzed the door. He then disappears out the door, leaving Rupert on his own. He starts to think about it for the first time since he got arrested about who could have possibly killed Jennifer. He's still in shock about the whole thing to be honest, because not twenty-four hours before he thought he had a second date with an amazing woman and was happy for the first time for a long time. The way his divorce played out he has found it quite hard to get back on his feet and it took him a long time to even think about dating again. It took some encouragement from his friends including Jason, which he took as an encouraging sign to eventually go on these apps and dip back in the world of dating. The door opens and Jason is stood there with a very unhappy Jess and Andrew, who looked a bit down beaten.

Jason leads them in and says with a stern face but Rupert can tell he is very happy, "So you're free to go," and turns to look at Jess who steps forward.

"Yes, Rupert you are free to go home but I still have to remind you that you are a suspect in this case and you are under strict instructions not to leave the county and we may call you back in for questioning, and due to the circumstances that the last IV ended in, there will be a mediator in the room with us."

"But that's only if you have sufficient evidence to bring my client back in," Jason chips in.

"Yes, that is correct," Jess says though gritted teeth.

"Right Rupert we are out of here. Thank you very much detectives, it's been wonderful," Jason replies with a bit of tongue in cheek. "Hopefully you won't need us back, can we please go and get Mr Graham's belongings from custody."

"Sure," Jess says. "Right this way," she says very short, and quickly spins and starts walking down the hallway.

Rupert feeling embarrassed by the whole situation, starts to make his way following Jess and Andrew.

Andrew hangs back to try and talk to Rupert, but with Jason not that far behind them, Rupert can see that Andrew is caught between saying something or keeping it unspoken. They walk in silence for a few moments, with Andrew deciding to not say anything.

They get back to the custody desk, where the sergeant who told Rupert to call Jason is waiting.

"Please can we release Mr Graham's belongings?" Jess says. The sergeant nods and heads off to the cupboard, she then turns to Rupert. "Can I ask something, Rupert?"

As he goes to say yes, Jason jumps in ahead of him "I don't think so, Detective, I think you have asked Rupert all you can ask him at the moment!"

Rupert shoots her an apologetic look; she looks back as though she's trying to look into his soul.

The sergeant returns and hands back everything to Rupert, naming it as he takes it out the box "One phone with scratched screen, one brown leather wallet and a set of keys with three keys on them. Please can you acknowledge that you have received the items with no damage and sign the form here please?"

Rupert signs and grabs his stuff of the desk, the relief to have his phone is palpable, it's just nice to feel a bit normal. He can see there's loads of message from work. He hasn't been able to tell them what's happening he thought he would be out by now and go to work without a problem, he will have to explain to them when he gets in later.

"Right thank you once again, officers," Jason says as he ushers Rupert towards the door. As they get towards the door, Rupert's thinks he hears a sudden load of people and as quick as a flash as soon as Jason goes to open the door, the light is blinding, a bit disorientated, he can hear questions being shouted at him from what seem like crowds all around him, things like "Are you a suspect in this case?" "Did you kill that woman?" "What's your name?" Just question after question being shouted at him.

He suddenly feels Jason pulls his arm towards him and hears him shout "NO COMMENT AT THIS TIME, CAN YOU LET US THROUGH, THANK YOU."

He realises like a freight train hitting him, that the bright lights and the questions can only be one thing. The press.

It's been released.

Chapter 21

Jess has just seen what has happened outside and is furious that this story has been released to the press. She storms back to her office and for the second time already today, she slams her office door. She walks over to her desk chair and slumps down into it, feeling defeated.

She's trying to think over everything that has happened since this case landed at her door. It feels as though they have been working on it for a lifetime but it's only been seven hours or so. There's a knock at the door.

She shouts, "Come in." the door opens very slightly and it's Dave who delivered this case this morning. She smiles warmly at him as her anger dissipates slightly. Dave's only been working here a few months, he's in training and is on the ball and is well on his way to being a detective when the time comes. He's known as Little Dave because there was already the other David. Jess didn't think it was fair at first but she has come to see him as the departments surrogate son and she makes sure the whole team looks after him. It's very easy to become so disillusioned in a job like this. She hates to see young recruits fall at the first hurdle. When she was training, she wished she had been looked after a bit more and been shown how to handle things. She was thrown in at the deep end on her first day as a detective. She was given a quadruple homicide where she wished someone had told her what she was going to see that day. If she wasn't so committed to being a detective, she would have left that day.

She had always wanted to be in the police from when she was about four, she used to have these little toy police cars that she used to act out scenes of car chases and robberies gone wrong, then when she was a bit older, she started doing murder scene with her toys and solving who did it. Her parents knew she was obsessed and tried to get her into other activities. They tried everything from horse riding to ballet, but every time she came back to the police, she just wanted to help people. She was an only child like her son at the moment. She wished she had a brother or sister she could chat to sometimes but her mum and dad have always made her feel so loved that she couldn't ask for better parents. They scrimped and saved to send her to university so she could study forensics, the day she left to start her course was difficult she had never been away from home and she went to what was then the best courses in the country up in Preston. They had the best facilities, they owned houses that could be used for a murder scene. Once she saw that, she had the time of her life there.

She had not long started her second year there though when the world dealt her a devastating blow, her dad became seriously ill with terminal cancer and after a few months of trying to fight it he sadly passed away before he got to see her achieve her dream. She tried to drop out but her mum wasn't having any of it. She's always admired her mum for that, putting her own problems behind her and to making sure that Jess finished her degree.

She has now repaid the favour and when she had enough money to buy a decent house, she made sure her mum rented out her home and came to live with her.

"Yes, Dave, what can I do for you?" she says, snapping out of her thoughts. "I just wanted to let you know that we are fielding a lot of press calls at the moment and I just wanted to know what you wanted to do."

She takes a moment and then thinks fuck it, she didn't want to do this but she's going to have to, her hand has been forced really. "Let's organise a press conference please."

"No problem will get on it at once." He goes to leave the room.

"Oh David!" she shouts through. "Have we found any relatives for Jennifer?"

"Oh yes, she has a sister that lives nearby. I've called her to come in, she should be here within the next twenty minutes."

"Excellent, please take her into one of the interview rooms straight away. I would like to talk to her about the press briefing before we do it."

"Sure thing, no problem," David says as he is leaving and shutting the door. Jess stands from behind her desk and goes towards the whiteboard that she frantically wrote the case on earlier. She always likes to do this, map it all out and she thinks the missing piece will appear.

There's another knock at her door. "Come in," she shouts.

It's John and David. "Ah guys, please come in, thanks for all the running about this morning, how did it all go?"

She always did this whenever one of her team comes back, she has a personal debrief with them, she feels that it allows her to understand the case first hand and not get it through Andrew, which is how the team used to work before she got promoted. When she was coming up through the ranks, she used to have to give everything over to Andrew who would then present it to the Chief. She always found the information was delivered differently, not given the airtime it properly deserved. So, when she became the Chief it was the first thing she changed. Now it works better she gets the info first hand and everyone feels as though their point has been heard. She leads them to her desk and sits down opposite them.

"It went really well," David leads. "The two interviews with the owner and the waitress brought up a lot of interesting information, some that we passed on straight away like the fact he was," David checks his note, "acting oddly and that it looked like he made an unwanted advancement. The waitress was under the impression that it went badly."

"Excellent work, guys, so from our end you've probably heard that when we pressed him on this issue, he had a panic attack and we had to stop the interview. He said that he had tried to touch her leg, thinking it was going well and she well told him off basically, but great work because it helped us get some more information about what happened last night. We are slowly filling in the gaps. John, do you have anything to add?" John looked up from his seat and flicked through his notes. "I don't think so, David led the interview, very well I might add." Jess looks over at David who is trying to stifle the pride he is obviously feeling for getting the praise.

"Excellent. Well done, David, and how did you guys get along with the CCTV?"

"So, we did a scope around the area and we have a list of various angles and we will start making our way through them bit by bit."

"Excellent, David do you mind going to a printing out an A3 sized version of the alley from above please?"

"Sure," David said jumping out of his chair and rushing to his computer.

"So, he did well?" Jess asks John, they have worked together for years. John is like Andrew, an old hand at this game and that's why she paired him with David, experience can't be taught but it can certainly help the newer ones look at things slightly differently than they have been told in training.

"Ah Jess, you've got yourself a great detective in the making there, might even replace you someday. He is precise, considerate and knows what to ask and what not to ask. I jumped in a few times but certainly far less than I have had to with some of the other recruits."

"That is amazing." She smiles.

David comes back into the room holding the freshly printed out map of the crime scene and puts it on her board. He then looks around and spots a Sharpie. "So, I found cameras here." He starts circling locations across the map. "And here and here." He then turns and hands the pen to John who then repeats the same speech for the cameras that he found.

Jess gets up and walks towards the board. "This is excellent guys; can we pull these three please," as she writes 1,2 and 3 next to them. "As soon as we can please."

"Will get on that straight away."

They leave her office. Her attention is drawn to the pictures of both of them and the location and she has now marked where each CCTV camera is She thinks the key has to be somewhere in here, it just has to be.

Chapter 22

I can't believe he's been fucking released! What the hell are they doing over there? I've given them more than enough to charge him. I've researched into Detective Chief Inspector Jessica Spears, with a reputation like that she should have had this case done and dusted within a few hours. Stupid bitch! Can't even solve a case that is laid out right in front of her.

The only thing that has perked my day up slightly is that the press was right there when Rupert got released. I had originally got them there to push the police into giving a press conference and forcing them to charge him to save face. But it all worked out in the end because now his face is plastered all over the news. I've been chuckling to myself looking over the pictures. That's the beauty of the press photographers doesn't matter how quickly you move your hand they always get your face. That stupid face deserves to be there for what he's done.

Ah! Live update. Please, please be a press conference! Fuck yes! They are called a press conference. I am elated – this pile on the pressure to charge him.

It doesn't matter anyway the thing about me is that I have many fires burning. Always have a back-up, that's my motto. So, Rupert if they don't have the fucking courage then you will have a world of pain coming your way. You don't do what you did and get away with it. When the truth comes out and it will come out everyone will see you for the lying pathetic mess you are. You will feel the fucking wrath of me.

The news conference starts in forty minutes I'm going to grab some popcorn and enjoy this!

Chapter 23

Jess looks up as there is another knock at her door just as she is finishing her statement for the press briefing. They're always the same, we are appealing for new information, we have a suspect but not charged anyone yet. It's Little Dave again, "Jess, I just wanted to let you know that Jennifer's sister is in Interview Room One and that the press conference is almost ready. Do you need me to print anything?"

"Excellent," she says and she gets up from her desk. "Yes, I've just saved a press briefing to the system. Do you mind printing it out for me and placing it in the press briefing pack please?"

"Absolutely!" Dave says with so much enthusiasm it's exhausting to watch, he then leaves the room and Jess gathers her notepad and case file and starts heading down to the interview room. Andrew looks up at her as she walks past "Do you need someone to come and sit with you Jess?" he asks meekly, probably hoping to get back in her good books she thinks.

"No, I'm all good, it's not a formal interview, I'm just updating her on the situation before we put it out for the entire country to see."

Andrew who looks disappointed, nods and then goes back to his screen. Jess thinks she should ask him to come along, she's feeling guilty about the way she talked to him earlier but he did cross a line and has potentially put a giant nail in this case. She thinks that it is time she starts acting a bit more like a boss and when shit hits the fan like it did today, she needs to stand firm. So, she carries on with her plan and makes her way down to the interview room. She always hates these conversations, it doesn't matter how many times she has had to do it, it always feels difficult. She remembers the first time she did this it was to a fifty-five-year-old man whose wife had just been killed in a hit and run. She can't remember his name; she finds that her mind blocks out personal details. All she can remember is the pure emotion that flowed out of him as his grief and life just all got laid on the table. She stayed with him for hours unable to leave just talking it all through, she got home and cried and cried and took it all personally. Since then, she has managed to detach herself from the situation and she doesn't stay as long, she tries tomkeep it very short and get in and out, it might seem cold to people on the outside but she can't keep piling the emotional stress on herself otherwise she would never make it. She breathes out and pulls the door open and sees a woman in her mid twenties who has some characteristics of the woman that Jess has been staring at on her board all morning.

"Hello, I'm Chief Inspector Detective Jess Spears. Thank you for coming in." She extends her hand.

"Becca," the woman replies. "Can I ask why I have been brought in? The gentlemen who rang me was very vague with the details and I feel like I'm not getting good news if I am here, has something happened?"

"Yes, I'm sorry about all the secrecy but I would rather do this in person." Jess notices Becca immediately looks nervous, but she proceeds.

"So last night at about 11pm, we were called to an incident at Barber Alley you know the cut through in town? When the officers arrived on scene, they found a woman in early thirties."

There it was she saw the horror flood over Becca's face. Jess calls it the moment, the realisation of the news about to come "I'm really sorry but the woman that was found was your sister, Jennifer."

"Oh my god, is she okay? Can I see her?" Becca pleads.

"I'm afraid that she had already passed by the time the officers arrived."

"No, No, No, that can't be true, that just can't be true!" Becca says, her eyes glossing over.

Jess takes a breath and continues "I'm afraid it is, I'm so sorry and I wish I had better news. But unfortunately, I have to tell you that this wasn't an accident, we believe she was murdered, I'm so sorry."

Now the grief hits, Jess thinks as she sees the bottom of Becca's eyes water. "That can't be right, there must be some mistake." Becca says her voice quivering as she says it.

"I'm afraid it isn't." She feels blunt for saying it but she has to make sure the message comes across clearly "She was on a date with someone she met online and we are currently investigating this individual, I wanted to get you in to tell you as we are about to do a press conference so I wanted you to be well informed before you hear anything that comes as a surprise, are there any other family members that you want to contact before we do this press conference."

Becca just sits in silence for a few moments, Jess can see all the thoughts racing through her head trying to take it all in. She knows what it's like to suddenly have that pain and grief thrown at your door, she had the same thing when her dad died. All she could hear for hours was white noise, as though the earth just stopped for an afternoon and she was on another plane of existence.

"Umm no, there isn't, our parents died in a car crash when I was fifteen and Jennifer was twenty-one. She was all I had," Becca says in a way that the words are coming out but she isn't thinking of what they are saying sort of way.

"Would you like a moment alone, or I can get one of our counsellors in? They are very good and it can always help to talk to another person especially when you have had news like this."

Becca suddenly just crumbles and puts her head in her arms and starts crying uncontrollably. Jess is in two minds – one half of her that is a mother just wants to care for the girl and put her arm around her but the police side of her knows that as soon as she lets in that emotional baggage, it's just going to make this case a lot harder because it then becomes emotionally involved.

She knows what's best but she can't stand to see people upset so she pulls up a chair and puts her arm around her "I'm so sorry." she says, she finds these situations she doesn't need to say very much, just being there sometimes can help.

While Jess is holding Becca, Andrew is busy just down the hallway helping to sort out the press conference, it's the least he can do after fucking up the interview earlier, he knows that. He could see the disappointment in Jess's face, they have been friends for years but he knows that when it comes to drawing a line and giving a bollocking out, that friendship takes a back seat. "Ladies and gentlemen, can I have your attention please?" He announces to the crowd of journalists that has now gathered in front of him.

"We will be beginning in about twenty minutes so if you can all just hang tight that would be great. Help yourself to tea and coffee." He points to the table that has been set in the corner that now houses two urns that look like they have been bought out for these things since the 80s. "Thank you very much." And with that he exits the room and hopes that this press conference goes well, it has to.

It's been fifteen minutes of non-stop crying from Becca and she has now entered the numb stage, Jess has seen it time and time again. When the body has no more left to give. Jess lingers a minute before she moves to the other side of the table "I'm very sorry for what has happened to you and I promise you we will bring the person who has done this to justice, the suspect that we are focusing on was found crouched over the body." Becca brings her hand up to her mouth in shock. "I don't want this to come across blunt but I have to give you the facts so that nothing is a surprise when we release our press statement. The person that was crouched over her was the individual she was on that date with." Becca looks up at her.

"That makes no sense," Becca says trying to compose herself

Jess feeling intrigued, "I know that it's hard to accept this news but they are the facts."

Becca has a puzzled look on her face "No I get that, what I don't get is that I spoke to my sister last night after the date. That was one of the conditions of her going for the date, it was probably a two-minute conversation but she sounded super happy about the date, not someone who could have potentially murdered her minutes later."

Jess mentally makes a note of this to ask her team to look into Jennifer's phone records for this, but she knows in her heart of hearts that she can't make it look like this information has come as a surprise. "I know it's difficult to understand but the truth is that sometimes you don't know who is sitting opposite you."

"Who is the guy?" Becca says pleading

"I really can't say, I wish I could but with an active investigation ongoing I'm afraid I can't." As Jess is saying this there is a knock on the door. "Come in."

Andrew opens the door. "Jess can I just have a word please."

"Yes sure, no problem just give me a minute and I'll be right out," Jess says to him and turns back to Becca "I'm so sorry for delivering this news and I'm sorry I can't give you any more answers for now but I'm really hoping that we are going to have some justice for you soon, but please ,if you need anything, give me call." She writes down her number and passes it across the table. "Anytime, day or night I'm always available, but stay here as long as you like, there's an officer outside who can escort you out when you are ready, I know it's a lot to take in, so I just want you to leave when you are ready." She gets up from the table her mind has already left the room with racing thoughts about the press conference and trying to predict what the questions are.

"Thank you, Detective," Becca says.

"Please, call me Jess." She holds her hand out which Becca receives and they shake hands. Jess then leaves the room and starts walking down the hall towards Andrew.

"Sorry I didn't mean to disturb but the press conference is ready for you."

"No need to say sorry. I needed an exit as harsh as that sounds but I never want to get pulled into the grief, makes the case harder to look at with fresh eyes, While I remember, she just said that her sister called her straight after the date. Can we just confirm that? The sister is under the impression the date ended well, which would fit with Rupert's version, but you never know."

"No problem, I'll get the team on it." They start walking down the hallway.

"Oh shit!" Jess says spinning round with some urgency and rushing back the way she came. Fuck, fuck, fuck she thought as she ran back down the hall way. She gets back to Interview Room One and opens the door and she sees Becca still sat in the same position and the folder with all the press notes and case notes on the table opposite still in the same place she had left it.

"So sorry just need to grab my folder," she says as Becca looks up as she backs her way out of the room and runs back down the hallway where she catches up with Andrew "Fuck that was close, so busy thinking about the press conference I forgot the fucking folder with everything in."

They arrive at the door that the press is currently waiting on the other side of. Jess takes a deep breath and opens the door.

Chapter 24

The room is filled with the noise of journalists chatting, catching up with each other, swapping stories, but as soon as they notice Jess has walked in, they fall silent. She often thinks that they are like a pack of lions that have just spotted a gazelle. She carries on her walk on to the little stage that has been set up. Every eye in the room is following her. As she arrives at the stage and approaches the mic, the usual photo-taking starts. After years of doing this she still hasn't got used to the flashes, she thought over time you would be able to ignore them but they still affect her.

"Good afternoon," she says as the mic crackles from the speakers dotted around the room. "Thank you for coming, I will now read a short statement and then we will go to questions." She looks around making sure that they have all heard. "At around twenty-three hundred hours last night a woman was on her way home from a date where she was attacked and murdered in the vicinity of Barber Alley. We are currently pursuing a suspect who was found at the scene of the crime, I want to stress that this individual has not been charged but is still under investigation. We believe that the woman who was in her early thirties had left the Italian restaurant in town and made her way down the hill before taking a short cut through Barber Alley. We then believe that she was attacked from behind and then tragically strangled. When the paramedics turned up, she had unfortunately passed away, this is a difficult and brutal crime. I have called this press conference to one get the facts out because I understand that there have been several posts on social media surrounding this case. I would also like to appeal to anyone who was in the restaurant or in the vicinity of the area around this time last to come forward, because any information no matter how big or small is can be very important. Thank you." Jess looks around the room "Any questions?" The lights light up on her lectern in front of her. They had this system installed during the high-profile case of the serial killer that saw her career take off, it enables them to see who wants to ask questions, instead of everyone shouting at once. Fortunately, it's not the main UK press today, it's just local press but that doesn't mean that it won't get picked up. "Yes, Dave Beadly, from *South Today*."

"Hi," Dave says in a curt way. "Can I ask, are you going to be releasing the name of the victim to aid this investigation as sometimes a picture can jog people's memory?"

"Thanks, Dave, not at this moment in time I think because of the tragic nature of this crime, for respect of her family I don't think it would be right to release that information right now. Fiona from the *Winchester Daily*."

"Thank you, Detective, if you have a suspect why have they not been charged? What are you holding out for?"

"I don't think we are holding out on anything. The suspect we had in questioning was released without charge but is still very much under investigation, we have a huge team working on this case and we are gathering evidence which should hopefully lead to a conviction in the next few days, although I can't promise you anything. I will also just mention before this question comes up, we will not be releasing the suspects name, I know that a lot of people will want to know but for the time being they are still under investigation. Corine *Meridian News*."

"Thank you, can you explain how this information has become leaked on social media and created a bit of a panic?"

"The leak is being internally investigated right now and we are shutting down every account that is tweeting details about this case and trying to close in on the source, the reason we have called this press conference is because we don't people to feel panicked and we want to assure people that they are safe and every resource is being used in this case, we are committed to finding the killer. Final question Joseph from Hampshire Radio."

"Thank you, Detective, I just wanted to ask are there any other suspects at this time and if there aren't why has this individual been released?"

Jess hates when this happens when they phrase a question slightly differently to another journalist to see if they can get another answer, fortunately with her press training she doesn't get so tripped up with these sorts of question like she used to.

"As I said to Fiona, the suspect has been released but is still very much under investigation and will be brought back in for questioning when the time is right to conclude this case, as for your question before there are no other suspects at this time but as I said we are appealing for information from anyone that knows anything. Thank you for all your questions, we will call another press conference when we have some more information but for the time being please allow us to carry on our investigation. I would just like to say what happened last night is a brutal and unacceptable crime, and the perpetrator will be brought to justice. Our thoughts and prayers are with the victim's family. Thank you everyone." Jess steps away from the lectern and breathes a sigh of relief, short and sweet that's how she likes it. She never lets them get in too many questions, because the facts then start getting muddled, short precise and to the point that is what she likes to do.

As she leaves the room, leaving the press officer to sort out handing out the statements to be printed or broadcast.

She heads back to her office and she is actually excited to get back in there, she always finds comfort in her office, it's her safe space and where she can think clearly and try to uncover what is lying in this case. She knows that it is right in front of her, but she just needs to connect the dots. She checks her watch; it's getting on for six and on a normal day she would be heading home right now to see her wonderful son who always makes her day feels better.

When cases like this come about, she knows that she won't be going home soon, which makes her feel sorry for her son, she thinks she is being a bad mum by not being there every night, but one thing that keeps her going through these difficult cases is that she is creating a safer future for him to grow up. She sometimes has the same reoccurring nightmare that she has to sit down and have the conversation with her son, who asks her in her innocent voice "How come they got away with it, Mummy?" and Jess has to explain that "Sometimes things don't always go our way and people get away with doing horrible crimes." To which her son looks disappointed and starts crying and crying and crying and she can't do anything about it. She often awakes from these dreams screaming out, often shocking her mother who is just next door, who rushes in as she did when Jess was a child and holds her until she feels better again. She doesn't know what she would do without her mum, she is the rock that keeps them all sane in that house and when cases come around like this, Jess is safe in the knowledge that her mum will look after him and will take the stress away so she can carry on. She wishes she was home but she needs to solve this case. She draws her attention back to the whiteboard in the corner of the room. That nugget of information is there, she can feel it in her bones.

Chapter 25

John and David watch as Jess heads into her office after the press conference, they know that when that happens, she just needs to be left alone. They have been busy working though the CCTV that they had identified and chatted through with Jess. David hates this part of the job, it's so minds numbing, just hours after hours of looking at the same black and white footage of the same street.

His eyes are burning from watching the screen intently but he knows that it needs to be done. He's not alone in it either, John is also along for the ride, he's done this a thousand time before. He is an expert, which is why they have been tasked with this job. John once solved a murder back in the early 90s from CCTV, nobody else spotted the figure far in the distance heading towards the house that ended up with an entire family getting murdered after a robbery went wrong.

John shouts over the computer opposite "Have you found anything yet, Dave?"

"Nothing, have you?"

"So, from the restaurant I have found Jennifer and Rupert saying goodbye, come and have a look at this?"

Dave gets up from his desk, his back stiffening as he does, after being hunched over the computer for hours. He stretches his arms out and walks around the desk and peers at the image on John's computer. There frozen in time is the moment Rupert and Jennifer say goodbye.

"Now you tell me, does that look like a date that has ended badly to you?" David watches the screen as John presses play and watches the two ghostly figures, appearing to be laughing on screen and then they pause for a second. John hits pause.

"Now what you are seeing there is two people who were laughing and joking. Now look carefully."

He hits play again and they are just stood there for a few seconds. John hits pause again and turns to look at David, with that look of, did you see that? "Watch it again," John says after getting the hint that David didn't see what he had seen.

Again, the figures just stand there for a few seconds. John pauses again. "I'm sorry, John, I don't see what's happening."

John looking confused at him points at the screen. "You see that little bit of light there that is a phone screen, If I had to put my money on it. I would say that they are exchanging a date and time for their next date, that doesn't look like it has gone badly at all."

"But the waitress and the owner of the restaurant said they thought it went very badly," David replies.

"Well, I don't know but there's something not right because CCTV doesn't lie, look at the body language, the way they are standing, it doesn't look like someone who is potentially afraid or pissed off at him."

"I just don't know what they would gain out of saying the date went badly."

"That is the question isn't it?" John says, David can tell he is pumped up at finding this bit of information. David walks back around his desk and starts looking at a different angle this time the camera is pointing away from the crime scene. He starts fast forwarding the footage the little counter in the corner getting closer and closer to the time of the crime. Something catches

David's eye as its rushing through, he rewinds it and watches again this time at normal speed. Looking up from over his desk, he shouts at John.

"John! Come here I think I've found something interesting."

Chapter 26

Isabella and Olivia have just managed to get away to visit the autopsy, it took forever for the scenes of crime officers to finish up. Olivia knows that they have to be precise but it started to feel it was taking the piss. What was good news was that they had successfully extracted a footprint and sent it off to the lab, which was going to take a few days to get back but the guys were pretty sure they should be able to get back some solid evidence.

They drive in silence for most of the journey, normally they can't stop talking but something about today has drained them. I think it's the fact that the woman who was murdered was not that far off their age, and it's always the same thing when something like that happens it makes them think about their own life and how short it can be.

"So, do you think he did it?" Isabella says to her while looking out the window. She's been asking this question at different points to the day, it's always a question that comes up on cases like this.

"I don't know to be honest; I think with cases like this there is always a detail that can be easily overlooked, I remember a case when I was back up in London, there was a case that came up when the evidence that the case hung on was a tiny strand of hair that was found on the victims belt loop from where the suspect tried to hold them down."

"Let's hope this autopsy shows something up, I have a feeling that if we don't find something else Jess is going to come down on us like a ton of bricks," Isabella says turning towards her. As Olivia is about to say something back the satnav chimes in and tells them to turn left.

Olivia turns into the car park as they switch the engine off the radio news comes on and they just catch Jess announcing about the case. As they get out of the car Olivia looks at Isabella. "Yeah now that's it out in the press the pressure is only going to get worse."

They walk into the autopsy office, the smell of this place always gets to Olivia, so metallic, she often thinks it smells of rust which she knows is an illusion but it makes her feel sick every time. Thank God the hangover has passed, she thinks to herself.

The pathologist on call today is Dr Andrew Bland who Olivia has gotten to know quite well over the last couple of months, they get on quite well but he is a very matter of fact. The first time she came across him, he told he in a very graphic way about how her victim had died. "So are you here to talk about the strangulation case that came in last night. She's over here." He points toward the table in the far corner. They walk over to the table covered in a sheet, he pulls back the sheet and reveals Jennifer. The first time Olivia saw a dead body it really stuck with her, but over time she doesn't see a being who hours earlier had been a living breathing person she now sees them as just a case and she detaches herself now. It's the easiest way.

Jennifer looked scared, her eyes were staring up as though she had seen a ghost and the marks around her neck were horrific. Her entire neck was black and blue. Olivia thinks to herself that there was some force that was needed to do that and as if reading her mind Dr Bland says, "Yeah that is some force needed to do that."

Isabella nods in agreement.

"So, can you tell us what you found from the autopsy?" Olivia asks. Picking up his folder he starts looking through the notes "So we have a thirty-one-year-old female whose cause of death was suffocation." Isabella takes out her notebook and starts writing. Andrew carries on. "The time of death was between eleven p.m. and twelve a.m. last night. If you look to the back of her head here." He picks her head up like how someone would pick up a football that's just rolled into the back of goal and points to a deep cut at the back of her head. "You can see a cut at the back of her head, this is where I believe she was attacked first. Looking at the trauma I would say she was pulled backwards and she hit her head on the pavement. I would then say that if you look here." He pulls up her top and then is two bruises at the bottom of her ribs. "This is where I believe the attacker sat on her while they were straggling them."

Olivia looks at the bruises. "So, are we thinking this is a man who's done this, it must have been some weight?" Andrew looks over at her. "Well you would think that but if you got on top of me now and sat and strangled me. It takes roughly a minute to strangle someone, and with the amount of pressure that is needed to strangle someone, the pressure has to go somewhere so naturally you would put all your weight through your knees to help ground you, so it can easily be a man or a woman, it's very difficult to say at this stage." Isabella and Olivia look at each other with a moment of despair.

"I'm guessing that's not the answer you wanted but I don't really want to say one or the other because it could be anyone's guess."

Olivia looks at him "Our suspect is male so it would have

helped to know if only a man could have done this."

"I'm sorry I can't give you any more than that, one last thing that I would like to show you before you go. If you look here," he points to Jennifer's neck, "the victim was strangled using black rubber gloves, because in cases like this when you strangle someone and you are using your bare hands, as I said there's a lot of force, it leaves tiny little indents of the pattern of your skin and sometimes very faint fingerprints, but here you can't see any of that and I found tiny particles of black residue."

Olivia and Isabella look at each other with the exact same thought, Rupert wasn't wearing gloves when he was arrested and none have been found on scene.

Chapter 27

I can't say I'm surprised that they didn't release his name. They are such fucking cowards but I can't get bogged down with the details. The main thing is that the case is out there and you are one step closer to be outed. It's going to be like all Christmases, birthdays and anniversaries all rolled into one. When you did what you did it. It affected everyone around you, but you managed to walk away unscathed, even though it was your fucking fault.

God! Every time I think about it makes my fucking blood boil, the day it happened was probably one of the worse days of my life. I was just happy going about my day and then, Bang! Like a freight train it happened! I couldn't believe it. I could have killed you on the spot. I even had it all thought out, I would buy a gun and walk over to your flat, knock on the door and as soon as you opened the door, I would hold the gun up in your bastard face and watch the fear come over you as you understand what is about to happen and then pull the trigger and BANG! It would have been over like that. Justice fucking served!

I went as far as getting the gun, its surprisingly easy. When I went to the shop, I was met by someone who was obviously a university student, just trying to make a few quid during the holiday. They asked my name and address which I gave them a name of a colleague who that I knew if they ever they did a background on would turn up nothing but I honestly don't think that kid even put it through, I thought he would say that I would have to wait two weeks which I had prepared myself for, but he didn't he just literally handed over the gun and the six bullets, although I only needed one for what I was planning.

When I got it home, I was so excited. It suddenly felt real and I was more convinced of my plan than I had ever been before. The gun felt heavier than I thought it would it, it also looks so light in the movies. Having it my hand I have never felt more powerful, I almost got in the car and went straight to you and did it right then. On the day I was going to do it, I got in the car and was driving over to your flat. The gun was in the glovebox ready and loaded, but when I got outside your flat, I sat and waited for an hour waiting for the right moment when I had an epiphany, why would I shoot you after what you did, Death for you is an easy way out if I was going to do this right you needed to suffer! So that's when I came up with this plan.

I am happy knowing that if this plan fails which I am nearly 100% sure it won't I have the gun as back-up! And click! There goes the next part of my plan, let's hope this speeds it up, Justice is coming for you Rupert and it's going to be a bitch!

Chapter 28

Rupert has just got home after being dropped off by Jason. He is so happy to be home, he puts the key in the lock and opens the door to his flat. He's only been living here a few months. In the divorce, they couldn't come to an agreement on who should get the house. He loved that house and it was the first house they had bought when they got married, back when life was simpler and they were in fully wedded bliss, he wished that it hadn't gone the way it did. It started the same way every divorce does, they both said it would be amicable but as soon as they got the big stuff such as the house, cars etc. that was when it went bad It then took months to decide anything. It turned into who could out stubborn the other. With the house, Rupert offered to buy her out of it because he loved it that much. He had done it up in between jobs so it was very much his passion project and to be honest he didn't want to let it go as it took him a long time to accept that they wouldn't be getting back together, he had thought about it and was hoping they could connect but it became apparently obvious half way through the divorce proceeding that there was no love left between them. This meant accepting that the house had to go. They both got an equal share but with the lawyer's fees, he didn't use Jason because he thought it would be a conflict of interest, he only had enough to buy this one bedroom flat. Even though it's small he's made it his own, he had hated it at first, the stupidly small kitchen that he gets frustrated every night because even though he is cooking a meal for one the worktops up fill so fast but stepping in it now after the night he's had, he's so happy to be home. He feels safe. Chucking his keys on to the side, he slumps down on the sofa. He picks up his phone and without thinking he heads to the police website where they are streaming the press conference. He doesn't want to watch it but curiosity is getting the best of him he needs to know what they say about him.

He sits and watches as Jess says that they won't name him and he can't help but feeling a little relieved, he feels incredibly guilty for thinking it but he knows that he had nothing to do with it, so he can't feel guilty.

As soon as the press conference is over, he immediately starts looking through the comments. He can't believe the filth that he reads from some people, saying that whoever has done this deserves to die and she got what was coming to her. He knows it's doom scrolling but he can't help himself. He finds that he needs to know what people think and even though his name is not released, he thinks that if they go ahead and charge him, it will be. Then those comments are all going to be about him and he sits there for about twenty minutes just thinking this is all because of a fucking mistake. He was just trying to help. He wished he hadn't turned around when he heard that scream as bad as that sounds. He imagines how it would have gone which would have been is that he was questioned and then as soon as they figured out, he was at home. It would have been over just like that. After forcing himself to put his phone down and the relief of his name not being used, he decides to try and get back to some sort of normality and thinks ahead to making some dinner.

A couple of hours later, Rupert is starting to feel better having finally had some decent food. His phone starts ringing on the other side of the room, his heart sinks, it can't be good news. His brain runs through a mental list of who the hell it could be at this time of night but his panic is soon put at ease as he sees the name "mum" flashing up on the screen. He was meant to call her hours ago and let her know what had happened.

"Hi, Mum," he says trying to sound cheery and as though he's not just spent the last few hours being questioned over murder; he knew he would have to say something because he can't keep something this big back from her. He just wants to protect her, because it's only been a year since his dad died. His mum completely fell apart, they had been together a long time and they were only a few months away from spending retirement together when he had a heart attack. They were all devastated. She is a bit better these days but Rupert spent most of the weeks following the funeral staying over at his mum's, taking care of her and making sure she was okay. Now she might have to be the one who takes care of him again.

"Hi, sweetie, how was your day? How was work today?" she said.

"It was okay, mum." Annoyed at himself for not saying anything, he needs to just tell her.

"Ah that's good swee…"

"Mum, sorry it wasn't okay. I have some bad news," he said trying to make it not sound as horrendous as it is.

"What is it, you're worrying me."

"You might see something on the news about a woman that was murdered last night," he says with some trepidation.

"What's that got to do with you?" There's a worried tone in her voice. He thumps his hand on the table in frustration, he doesn't want to tell her, but he knows he has too.

"I was on a date with the woman who got murdered," he says

holding his breath.

"Oh my god! Rupert!"

Taking a deep breath, "That's not the worst part, Mum." He hears her stifle. "I was found crouched over her body, I'm currently under suspicion for her murder." He finishes talking and doesn't hear anything, there's an uncomfortable silence between them. He suddenly feels very alone and feels like his apartment swallowing him whole, then he hears the saddest sound, heavy breathing down the phone and he knows that his mum is crying. "I'm so sorry, Mum, I didn't do it! I promise!"

"I wish your dad was here," she says in between the tears

"Me too, Mum, I wish I could just talk to him one last time," Rupert says with a heavy heart. He knows even his dad wouldn't know what to do in this situation.

After about ten minutes of her crying down the phone, she finally says, "So what happens now, are they arresting you?"

"They haven't charged me but I'm still under active investigation while they look for evidence. Please believe me mum, I didn't do this. The whole thing is a huge misunderstanding, I was just in the wrong place at the wrong time."

"I believe you," she says, and for the first time today he can hear that someone actually does.

"You have no idea how nice that is to hear," he says in relief and his eyes start to well up, it hasn't felt real until now. Talking about it outside of the police station has made it feel like it is actually happening and he's not watching some sort of movie that is playing out right in front of his eyes.

"Just stick to the facts son and it will show you didn't do it. Have you got a lawyer or do you want me to recommend one? I'm pretty sure your dad's old lawyer's firm is still going. I can put in a call if you want me to?"

"No, it's okay, Mum. I have Jason helping me."

"Oh." He always gets the same reaction whenever he mentions either her name or one of her family, it's always the same tone. His mum loved Steph and had treated her like a daughter, she had been in their lives for so long that she was part of the family and when the divorce happened it was like losing part of it. The betrayal and the trust that was broken still sits bitter and deep within Rupert's mum.

"He's a great lawyer, Mum, and has been really good to me since the divorce happened, we haven't let it ruin our friendship."

"I'm sure he is, son, but just be careful."

"I will mu…" suddenly Rupert's phone starts going mental in his ear, message after message after message. Notification after notification after notification. It's like his phone has become some sort of hotline. A call then comes in from a number he doesn't know, he lets it go to voicemail and as soon as it clicked off, it comes through again. He can't ignore it

"I'm really sorry, Mum, I'm going to have to go. I'll call you straight back, someone is trying to call me."

"Okay sweetie, and remember what I said be careful. I love you."

"Love you too, Mum." He puts the phone down and immediately answers the other number.

"Hello."

"Hi, this is Fiona from the *Winchester Daily*, can I get your comments about you being investigated for murder?"

Panic suddenly cries out in his head. His name has been leaked to the press.

PART 2

Chapter 29

1 Week later

Jess's alarm bolts her awake she picks up her phone and squints at the time. 4.30 a.m. It's been a week since Rupert's name has been released and the pressure on her and her team has gone up exponentially. The night it happened; she just couldn't believe it. She had been sat in her office going over all of her notes when there was suddenly a flurry of panic outside in the main room. She saw the whole team talking to one another in hushed tones. She thought they had come across a new piece of evidence; she went out there and asked. As she looked at each one of their faces, she knew it wasn't good news.

"What's happened?" she asked in a concerned tone.

Andrew spoke in a very sorrowful tone. "I'm afraid, Jess, that Rupert's name has been leaked to the press, it turned up on a Twitter account about half an hour ago, it sent out forty tweets each one tagging a newspaper in it, local and national. It has since been deleted but not before every paper has picked up the story."

Jess is devasted and wants to scream "Fuck sake!" she says and turns around and grabs a folder off the desk and throws it across the room. "How has this happened? It must be someone internal. Who else knows his name and why on earth would they want to release it?"

"I'm not sure, but we have the IT guys trying to track it down but apparently every tweet was sent from a different IP address. Whoever did this certainly know what they were doing," Andrew says.

"Of course, they know what they are doing the fucker has been one step ahead the entire time."

John suddenly outbursts, "I fucking hate social media, it was never like this before, you could just get on with your business and solve a case without every Tom, Dick and fucking Harry announcing it to the world."

At this moment Little Dave comes up to Jess. "Jess, I've got Rupert Graham's lawyer, Jason, on the phone. He sounds angry."

"Oh, great that's all I need that," Jess replies looking at Dave who regresses slightly as though he's been told off. "Just put him through to my office. Right," she says turning back to the team. "This is going to put this case on a pedestal and we need to knock it off. This is a massive set back but we need to solve it so everyone get back to what you were doing and ignore all calls you get from your press friends!" she says even though she thinks that it has made this case much harder to solve, because once it's out there suddenly a lot of false testimonies come from people who just want their fifteen minutes of fame. As she went back into her office, she picks up the phone to Jason "WHAT THE FUCK HAVE YOU DONE? WHY HAS RUPERT'S NAME BEEN RELEASED?" He screamed down the phone at her.

"Jason, we didn't leak this. No one in my team has leaked this."

"Well, someone has! This is fucking disaster."

Jess has to really hold her tongue, and stop herself from saying that if Rupert just admitted it, all of this would be over, but she takes a breath. "Listen Jason, I promise you that nothing has come from our end and we are doing all we can to solve this case and either charge your client or drop the investigation."

"Well, I suggest, Detective, that you look at your team a lot more closely because someone has leaked it. I don't know what sort of operation you are running over there but if this isn't sorted soon and keeps dragging out over you and your team's incompetence then I assure you a giant fucking lawsuit will be heading your way."

And with that there's a click and the phone goes dead. Jess sat in her office for a good hour fuming over the phone call until Andrew came in and said to her that she should really go home, she protested and said she was going to stay but he pretty much shooed out the door. When she got home her son was waiting for her, he had refused to go to bed until she had seen him. She read him a bedtime story and for brief ten minutes she was just having fun reading a story, and doing silly voices and laughing away, she didn't worry about the case or anything until the bedroom door shut.

When she got back downstairs, her mum had made her dinner, and even though she wasn't that hungry she couldn't say no to her mum and started eating and immediately felt a bit better. Jess and her mum chatted for about an hour that night about the case and her mum didn't say anything, she just let Jess talk and at the end it she said the best thing that Jess had heard all day. "Jess, my darling, I could tell you a thousand times over not to stress about this or don't work too hard and don't stay late, but I know you won't listen. So, all I'm going to say is this – I believe that you will solve this case and I'm proud of you no matter what happens, sweetheart."

She's thought of it a lot since that conversation and it's helping her stay strong and keep going. She's been at the office non-stop since Rupert's name was released, the new information that her team got, pushed the case in a different direction. The gloves theory that her team have been working through the last week doesn't conclusively rule out Rupert because he could have disposed of them at any point from the murder to the police turning up, so they have been searching bins, waste sites and even the drains underneath the crime scene. She has a nagging feeling at the back of her mind that Rupert is telling the truth but she's not saying anything because they need hard evidence that it isn't him. As she creeps out of the house, and looks back at the darkness that shrouds it, she knows that it will be a while until she sees it in the daylight again. She feels hopeful as she starts the car and heads to the station. The killer, whether it's Rupert or someone else, has left something somewhere, they always do. As Jess says when she is trying to teach officers coming up through the ranks "No matter how much you think you have committed a perfect crime, there's always something that leads you to the criminal, no matter how small it is."

Chapter 30

Arriving at work Jess sees the clock on her car tick over to half five, she's just heard the news come across the radio as she was switching off the car, she usually likes sitting in the car for five minutes before she gets out and into work. She feels hearing the news just gives her a little glimpse of what's going on in the world and set her up for her day. Not today though, because when the headlines came on the first thing that was read out by the newsreader was "Coming up in today's news, the Barber Alley killer investigation, we ask the public how they are feeling about the investigation." Jess hears a teaser from a member of public who she thinks is probably someone who just wants their five minutes of fame "I think that the police are doing a horrible job, we need answers. The streets aren't safe until they have the killer." She switches it off after that she can't bear to listen it anymore and she can't let it cloud her judgement.

As she walks in, she doesn't do her normal good morning to everyone, she can't bear it, she just wants to get to her office as quickly as possible to look over the case reports for probably the hundredth time and she's eager to get the updates from the team overnight. The results from the footprint found at the scene should be being picked up by Olivia and Isabella on their way in. She doesn't even make it to her office before Andrew is right by her side. Usually in big cases she gets in earlier than everyone else and has minimum half an hour to herself before everyone starts knocking on her door but this case just feels different, it's got a lot of press coverage and has hit a point with the public about not being safe in the streets and she knows that they have someone who should be their killer but with the only evidence that they have is that he was there when they found him and different accounts of the date. Even with CCTV, they still don't have enough to charge him.

"Good morning," Andrew says, he's been trying to sound upbeat all week as though they are going to solve the case today but they both know that's not the case. "So, I just wanted to check in with you for when you want me to gather the team for the meeting this morning?"

"When is everyone in?" Jess asks, walking around her desk and sitting down in the chair.

"Well," getting his phone out, Jess knows that they have a WhatsApp group without her in it. She's sure they bitch about her, but she doesn't care, it enables her to delegate to Andrew and keep her distance from them as their boss. "David and John should be in any minute. They are still going through CCTV so they will be available whenever, same with Jamie and Ava, oh they are just walking in," he says as Jamie and Ava appear coming up the stairs and into the office in deep conversation as Jamie makes a gesture and Ava laughs as they are talking off their coats and sitting down at their desks. Jess knows that they had only just left last night when she had at eleven. "They are still doing the background checks so they again are available whenever. The only team that will be in a bit later is Olivia and Isabella as the lab that is dealing with the footprint analysis doesn't open until half eight so they won't be in until nine."

"Brilliant. I think as soon as they are in, let's have the meeting."

"No worries, will let them all know, is there anything else you need before the meeting?"

"No, just make sure all the teams have something to bring to the meeting please?"

"Will do." And with that Andrew left and shut the door. It's so nice to have a bit of peace and quiet to give her time to think. She sits back in her chair and stares at the whiteboard that she's been looking at, hoping an answer is going to jump out, when she notices something. She gets up from her desk and walks towards the map and looks at the circles of the CCTV that John and David drew over a week ago and she starts drawing lines out of the circles to indicate their point of view and she can see that from the restaurant to the start of the alleyway, she can see it's all covered until it reaches the other end where there seems to be a glaring hole of coverage. She's lived in this city for a long time and she knows that a few years ago they did a scheme where the council decided to offer local businesses a £1000 grant to get CCTV on their premises. It was a big push to make the city feel safer. They obviously got a bit of a backlash from some local residents saying the city was turning into big brother but overall, it did seem to make the city safer and crime started to decline. She can't possibly see why there wouldn't be a CCTV camera on a business down the road that faces the back of Barber Alley. After a quick Google search, she finds a list of businesses and lists them out, she's going to give them to David and John and get them to look at it, she's positive that there will be a camera there. Jess sits back down at her desks and starts looking back through the case notes, she thinks that if they can find even a shred of evidence it will lead them to someone, she's sure of it.

Chapter 31

While Jess is going over case notes and preparing for her meeting, Rupert is being woken up by his phone going off. It had been going non-stop when his name had been released by a Twitter account, which has now been deleted, but the last couple of days it's started to die down a bit. The moment it broke he rang Jason straight away who was fuming and said in a very of matter of fact tone down the phone "I'll deal with this," and hung up the phone. For the last few days Rupert has not left his flat, he has pretty much lived-in darkness because every time he opens a curtain even slightly, the press who have been camping outside his home for the last few days, started taking photos to even get a glimpse of him. What's worse is that since his name has been released a few national papers have picked it up, so there's been new reporters outside doing live reports that end up on the news every night. He's been dubbed as the Barber Strangler by some of the tabloids. Jason came around as soon as he could and was bombarded with questions as he waited for Rupert to buzz him into the building. It was then agreed from that day forward that Jason would have a key to the front door so he could get in with ease and speed, avoiding the hounding from the press.

He had been so good on that first day and calmly explained what they were going to do next which was just try to carry on as normal and that the truth would prevail and this will be no more than a distant memory. He explained that he had had a go at Jess, in his words, "I've tried to put the frighteners on them by threating a lawsuit." Rupert was just glad that he had his back. He had called his mum back on that fateful night his name was released and cried down the phone for a good hour. His mum was trying to be a supportive as she could be, but he could hear the worry in her voice. She said the same thing as Jason, "This will blow over, son, you're innocent remember that." He's been trying but it's very difficult when you feel like a prisoner in your own home. He thought, albeit naïvely, that when he was released that would be it and that he would be safe for a while.

He called into work sick for the next few days although he is sure they already know but he can't face them yet, he can't face anyone, he knew he would have to go in soon though as they were quickly approaching the deadline for the show they were making. As Rupert makes his way to the bathroom from the sofa that has been housing him for the last couple of days, he catches himself in the mirror and doesn't recognise the person staring back at him. Gone is the clean shaven, well-kept and well-dressed individual who a few days ago looked in this exact same mirror ready for the first date for a long time. He is now looking at a stubbly face with his hair all rough and ready and he's been in the same loungewear for the past three days. A knock at the door breaks his thoughts and he goes to open it and finds Jason stood there "Fucking hell, Rupert, you look awful" he says as he comes into the dark flat. "What did I say, you need to try and carry on as normal not turn your flat into a fucking pit!"

He goes over to the curtains and opens them to let light flood into the room. Rupert squints at the brightness "Right, the more you do this and stay inside, the more guilty you look. You need to act normal. Get dressed, mate."

"Why?"

"Because I think you need to go to work, it will keep your mind off this and keep you occupied. I'll help you get out of here, there's only a few press here today. It's Friday so they are all off doing puff pieces for the weekend, come on, you need this!"

Rupert looks at Jason and smiles, it's the first time he has smiled all week and there's something rousing about Jason that Rupert has always looked up to. He's got this drive and passion that rubs off on the people he's around and Rupert feels slightly better.

He goes to shave and have a shower for the first time in days. Jason's right, he needs to act normal and show he's got nothing to hide. After about twenty minutes he's back to being clean shaven and looking ready for the day.

When he steps back out into the lounge/kitchen area Jason smiles, "There we go, mate, thank God you've got me around, eh?" Jason extends his arms out and they hug. "You've got this! Right, I think the best way to get you out of here with no-one noticing is that you go out the fire escape on the ground floor and I'll go out the front and distract them for a moment while you get your car from around the back. How does that sound?"

"Sound like a plan to me," Rupert replies.

As they leave his flat and make their way downstairs, before they part Jason says "Good luck, I'm going to try and get an update and see what's going on with those monkeys down at the police station, I'm telling you they couldn't organise a piss up in a brewery some of that lot." With that he winks and they hug again. "You'll be fine, like I said, you've got this." Feeling reassured they part and carry out their plan. It works like a dream and Rupert makes it to his car without any trouble and starts the engine. Just act normal is all he is repeating to himself as he drives away. It doesn't take him too long to get into the office. He's never been this long out of the office before. He's thrown himself into work since his divorce, it's the only way he could cope with suddenly being on his own. He had been known to come in at 6am and stay until 11 pm. He had even bought himself a fridge for his office so that he could store dinners in there for the late evenings. He gets to his office after passing the receptionist and saying his usual good morning to her. She looked uneasy but he tried to ignore it. Stay normal, that's all he can aim for. He had been with the same company for a long time, he had worked his way up through the ranks from assistant producer to producer to series producer and just recently been promoted to executive producer, overseeing several of their productions. Both he and his wife had started at the same time and had both risen through the ranks around the similar time and they had loads of friends here, when she got promoted to executive producer she went off to a different company. Rupert was so supportive and encouraged her to go, it was too much of a good opportunity to turn down, that was when the problems started to happen. They started to spend more and more time apart due to work being so busy and they drifted apart, but he can't think about that now, he needs to crack on with work. It is soon proven that staying away for over week was a mistake, he opens his work laptop and he's got over a hundred emails to deal with such as scheduling reports, edit notes and contributor breakdowns. It feels so good to be back and he feels all his other problems slowly slipping away from his thoughts. What he doesn't notice is that everybody walking past his office is staring at him.

Chapter 32

The clocks just hit 9 am and Jess looks up from making her notes and questions for the catch-up meeting to see Olivia and Isabella walking in with the pack containing the footprint analysis and the report. She saw David and John come in about half an hour ago, both looking bleary eyed. She knows that looking at CCTV for hours and hours on end is exhausting but someone has to do it and unfortunately for David, John is excellent at spotting minute details.

She sees Andrew run over to Team C as soon as they are about to sit down and she can see they aren't best pleased about having to go straight into a meeting. She always gets the feeling that Olivia and Isabella work to their own pace. They hate being rushed and told what to do, but they work really well as a pair hence why she has put them together again. They are such good friends, they bounce off one another with ease. It took a few months for Jess to find the right pairings but in the end she's happy with them. She tried John with Isabella which lasted about a week as they didn't work that well as a team so went off and did their own thing which is not how Jess wanted them to work. When she paired John and David together, she could see instantly that they were going to work. David wants to learn and John is a sound teacher, whereas with Olivia and Isabella they work well when they collaborate. She sees Andrew usher them in and then grab the others and she makes eye contact with him through her office window and she nods and holds up one finger to say she will be with him in one minute.

Once she can see everyone is settled, she leaves her office and makes her way across to the meeting room. "Good morning everyone," she says trying not to sound as tired as she is. "Thank you for gathering. It's been just over a week since we have had this case can I get an update please? John and David, can you start? How are you getting on with the CCTV?"

David looks down at his notes. "Well we have been looking at every minute of the CCTV and it's looking more and more likely that the date ended well. We have tracked Rupert's movements to the start of Barber Alley which corresponds with his account of events but it doesn't prove that he's not the killer because the autopsy report that Olivia and Izzy brought back last week the time of death could be any when from the time Rupert enters that alleyway and unfortunately there's no camera's there. At the moment that's all we have. We are checking the other angles just in case there's more." Andrew looking up at David "Why do you think the date ended well?"

John chips in. "Because if you look at these images," he says as he passes around the still that he and David looked at the other week. "You can clearly see they have their phones in their hands, which means that when he said that they were trying figure out the next date, it is most likely true. Also, you can see that their body language is relaxed, she doesn't seem scared or angry in my opinion."

Jamie says looking the picture. "Then why would the waitress and the owner say it went wrong?"

"I don't know. Crossed wires? People sometimes remember the wrong things and sometimes you remember the feeling and not the actual context. We have been trying to get hold of the waitress to ask more questions but she has been dodging our calls and has called in sick to the restaurant apparently."

"That's brilliant work guys, thank you." Jess says "The CCTV, I want you to go along to these businesses." She hands over the note she made earlier. "I'm convinced there is a blind spot at that end of Barber Alley and I'm struggling to see why, when the rest of the city has cameras everywhere."

She sees David look sad at this news, she's sure he thought them looking at CCTV was over for now. "I know it's tough going through it but this footage could literally make or break this case and even if it's not Rupert, I bet my life that if there is another killer they entered from that end."

"No problem, we will check that out straight away," John says. "Thank you. Now Jamie and Ava, what have you found out?"

Ava gets up and makes her way around the room and passes out a few pages of A4 that have been stapled together. Jess has a brief look through them as Ava sits down and starts talking them through it, "So, as you see here this is a very brief background check on Rupert Graham. You can see that his divorce was listed as extra marital relations now we know that from the interview that Jess and Andrew conducted Rupert stated it was his wife that cheated on him and after some digging, we have found that to be true. She apparently, according to the court transcript from their divorce, went away for work and started a three-month long affair with one of her colleagues. There had been a huge number of problems at home between the two of them and she had had enough. She states that he was violent to her a few times, which he denied and when pushed she couldn't provide any evidence, so it was ultimately ruled out as a tactic to get more money from the situation."

"That is horrific," Olivia says. "As if that could have been a genuine thing, you know bruises heal, the fucking system is messed up."

"I know tell me about it." Ava carries on, "So we've tried to contact his wife to find out a bit more information. We haven't managed to get her on the phone but we've left a few messages now saying it's urgent and that she needs to call us. I don't get a great feeling from her, so fingers crossed we hear from her, and then the other background stuff we have done is look into his phone and text messages…" She turns and looks at Jamie, who picks up like a well-oiled double act, "which made for interesting reading if you turn to page two of the document, we have just handed out you will see the messages and I must warn you some of them are quite graphic."

With that Jess turns the page over and reads through the messages. They are graphic and reek of some who seems desperate for a date and some of them just seem desperate for sex. The whole team sits in silence for a minute and reads them. Once Jess has finished reading them, she says "Excellent work guys, this certainly helps us build a good character profile to work with. If you concentrate on the wife and find out more information from these women he's contacted that would be great." She turns to Olivia.

"So, Olivia and Isabella can we get the analysis for the footprint please?" She takes a seat as Olivia gets the notes ready and plugs her computer into the projector systems in the room, as her laptop image appears on the screen, Isabella gets up and switches the lights off to plunge the room into darkness. "So it's good news," says Olivia very confidently and brings up the image of the footprint sent form the lab "The lab found that the shoe was around a size eight and they think the individual might have been running towards the victim because as you can see here the front of the shoe has a deeper impact than the rear of the shoe, the lab said it was lucky that it had been dry that night because the mud that the footprint was in moulded perfectly." She looks around the room and clicks the next slide. "Now the lab said that the make of this shoe is really unique."

Jess's ears prick at the word. She interrupts, "How is it unique?" Olivia turning towards Jess. "Ah this is the good news, the lab said looking at the logo." She clicks forward and a red arrow appears pointing at the logo in the middle of the shoe "Seems to read ShoeState," Andrew interrupts this time. "ShoeState, why is that name so familiar, that's not a big brand is it?"

Olivia smiles. "No, it's not, they are a small independent shoe shop that only operates here, they don't sell brands, they only sell shoes that they make themselves, so that means that they could have only been bought here. Now the lab says that if you look at the tread patterns here." She clicks to the next slide which is a close up of the treads. "They aren't worn very much on either side." Jess's heart suddenly leaps "So does that mean?"

Olivia interrupts. "Yes, they are brand new and probably purchased within the last two weeks."

"That is great news!" Jess says finally feeling the good news, but then it is immediately dealt with another blow delivered by Andrew who also has the case report in front of him saying the words that made the whole team sit in silence. "But Rupert wasn't brought in wearing branded trainers."

Chapter 33

Rupert, who's been busy working through his emails while Jess and her team have been talking about him and discussing his life. He noticed as more and more people came in that they were staring into his office as though he was some animal at the zoo. He was trying his best not to get frustrated and trying to keep positive, but it was hard. These are the people he had known for years and they were all looking and talking about him in the context of a murderer. He wanted to go out into the main office and scream at the stop of his lungs that he was innocent. He just wants someone to believe him. He carries on and even goes and grabs a coffee to which they all stop talking as soon as he enters the room, he wants them to feel he's not bothered, even though he's deeply upset inside.

When he gets back to his office he settles back at his desk and starts responding to more emails and is deep in thought when there is a knock at his door, he looks up to see the creative director of the company, Stephen. He had known Stephen for years; he had given Rupert a break and got him his first producer job and then from then on, they have constantly worked together as they had both risen through the ranks of the company. They had been known to go out on very long and boozy lunches, and they regularly had dinner dates around each other's houses when Rupert was married. Stephen had even been there to pick him up when the divorce happened, helping him move and taking him out to keep him busy. They were truly good friends and Rupert was finally pleased to see another face who he knew would believe him.

"Morning mate, I'm surprised to see you in," Stephen says somehow managing to reference the news without actually saying it.

"Well, I have to keep busy and we've got a show to make, haven't we? just trying to get back to some normality and trying to put this behind me," Rupert says back to him hoping that he will just turn and leave him to it. "That's great, mate, do you mind if we have a meeting in my office in two minutes to discuss the show? You've missed a bit," Stephen says.

"No problem, just let me grab my notes and I'll be right in," Rupert says feeling the normality coming back.

"Great," Stephen says as he turns and leaves. Rupert grabs some things and heads over the Stephen's office which is across the open office from his. He notices people staring but tries to block it out. He knocks on the door and a muffled "Come in." comes from inside. As Rupert opens the door, he notices that this isn't just a meeting between him and Stephen. The head of legal, Susan, and the owner of the company, Rachel, are there waiting for him.

Rupert already feels a dread of fear washing over him.

"Thanks for coming over, Rupert," Stephen says, as he gestures to a chair next to Rachel. As Rupert takes a seat, Stephen's quick to jump in, feeling the awkwardness, "So I think Rupert we should just get straight into it. We have called this meeting because we have become aware of your situation and we just wanted to talk with you."

Rupert responds with an answer that he had already thought of on his drive to work. "I know that my situation is obviously not great right now, but it will not affect my work and I just want you to know that I am innocent, I have not done this and what has happened is just a misunderstanding."

Stephen looks at Rachel and then back across to Rupert "Look, Rupert, I know you say you are innocent but you are still under investigation and that's something we can't look beyond at the moment. We have to deal with this to save the reputation of the show we can't have a... a..."

Rupert hurt and angry responds because he can't believe what he is hearing these people are meant to be his friends and trust him "A what? What exactly do you think I am Stephen?"

"A potential murderer linked to the show," Stephen eventually says.

"This is absolute bullshit, I am innocent, do you not believe me?" Rupert says raising his voice slightly.

"It's not a case of believing you or not Rupert," Stephen replies. "It is, do you believe me?" Rupert says again.

"Mate, it's not..." Stephen starts to say.

"Don't mate me. I want to know if the people who I am closest to, who I work alongside every day, think I am a killer or not. It's very fucking simple! Yes, or no?"

Stephen looks down at his desk and Rupert can see exactly what he thinks, the word no is heavy and unspoken in the air, Rupert has completely forgotten that there are two other people in the room, his brain is firing thoughts around his head so fast that he can't comprehend that they don't believe him.

Rachel breaks his thoughts, "Rupert, listen to me, you have been a valuable asset to this company but over the last few months we have all become a bit worried about you, you haven't been yourself and we know you have been going through a lot but you hardly leave and you have become very insular and I'm sorry but I'm finding it very hard to believe you when you were found at the crime, you surely understand that, don't you?"

And with that, Rupert's emotions rush to the surface and tears form in the corner of his eyes. Without work he is nothing, it has defined him for so long and to hear someone who he had trusted for so many years turn around and say they don't believe him. With the tears running down his face he turns so he can talk to Stephen and Rachel at the same time. "Please, this is all I have left, I've lost everything else and the past few days have been really hard. I'll do anything to stay in this job. What about if I work from home so no one knows I'm still working? And then when all this is over and I'm shown to be innocent we can talk about me coming back."

Stephen looks at him and looks as though he is about to talk but can't get the words out when Rachel steps in. "Look Rupert, I don't think that would work, and I'm afraid we have made our decision." She looks at Stephen as if you say get a move on. He sits up straight and says, "So Rupert we have decided to end your contract early which is effective from today. I'm so sorry, Rupert, but we can't have your name associated with the show, it just can't happen." Rupert sits there, shocked and feels like his whole world has just fallen apart. He can't think straight. What the hell is he going to do now? His job was all he had left. Over the last few months, he had lost his wife, his home and now he's gone and lost his job all because of a misunderstanding "Please can you reconsider, I'll do anything. You can't do this."

Susan speaks for the first time since the meeting started. "I'm afraid we can. In your contract it states that for any reason if the contractor becomes involved in a legal case, we have the right to terminate your contract immediately and I'm afraid it already has been signed by the relevant parties." With this she pulls a piece of paper out of her folder and hands it over to Rupert. As he takes it, he can see that it is a termination of contract with his name written at the top and at the bottom he can see that it has been signed by Stephen and Rachel and then witnessed by Susan. His heart sinks. There is a long uncomfortable silence until Stephen breaks it. "I'm so sorry, mate, we had no choice, you've got to understand."

Feeling a sudden rush of anger. "Oh, I understand, I understand that the people who I thought always had my fucking back have turned on me and taken the coward's way out. Come on Stephen, we've been friends for years, you know me! You know that I wouldn't do anything like this! You have got to believe me."

"We have no choice. I'm still your friend and I do believe you but the show needs protecting we have lots of jobs to think about, you've got to understand."

"You're not my friend, a friend wouldn't do this, a friend would have stuck up for me!" Rupert says.

"Enough!" Rachel interrupts. "I've not come here to watch a spat between to friends. I'm here to protect the show and the company and right now Rupert, you are doing damage to both, so I'm afraid the decision has been made and you are just going to have to live with it. I'm sorry but that's the way it is!" Rupert takes a breath he's still angry but even he knows that shouting and screaming is not going to get him anywhere, he's just really hurt.

"Well after all this will I be able to come back?" Rupert asks Rachel, he can't even look at Stephen. "I'm afraid not, I think the reputation you would bring would always hang over the show, even if you were innocent."

Rupert looks at the floor, he can't believe this is happening, then the biggest blow of all is delivered by Rachel "Also we are about to release a statement to the press regarding your termination."

"What? Why would you do that, why would you just not let me go?" Rupert asks.

"Do you realise how many journalists have been calling us daily since your name was leaked to get a story or try and name us in your story? A lot! And this was the only way we can distance ourselves from you Rupert, I'm sorry." Stephen says. Rupert puts his heads in his hands and sits hoping this is a bad dream; he's been doing that a lot lately but it's not working he is living this reality.

Rachel who seems happy that now this business is done like a leak on a ship being repaired, gets up, "Thank you for your time Rupert and I'm sorry it has come to this. Good luck with everything. We will give you a moment to gather your things and then security will see you out." And with that she leaves the room, closely followed by Susan. Rupert looks at Stephen in disbelief.

"I'm sorr…" Stephen starts to say

"Don't you fucking dare say you're sorry again," Rupert says as he heads towards the door. "You know I thought we were friends but I guess we were just work colleagues, because someone who has spent as much time with me as you should know that I have not done this, so thank you 'friend,' not only have I been fired from a job I have poured by heart and soul into, one of my closet friends has fucked up my entire career because nobody will hire me now will they, once that press release hits the papers."

"I'm not the one who has been fucking found crouched over a dead body, that quite frankly looks pretty fucking suspicious.

I've read all the stuff in the paper, there's been reports that you sent creepy texts to women on Tinder. I don't recognise the person I'm reading about so maybe you are right, maybe we are just colleagues who were close! This was not an easy decision so DON'T YOU DARE MAKE IT SEEM LIKE IT WAS." Stephen replies raising his voice so loud that everyone out in the open office stops working and looks towards the windows. "You believe all that shit in the paper then you are dumber than I ever thought," Rupert replies.

"Just leave, Rupert!" Stephen says sitting back down at his desk, with nothing more to say Rupert opens the door to find two security men waiting for him. He doesn't even look back at Stephen, he just leaves as the security escorts him across the room. If he thought he had been looked at before he now had every eye in the room on him.

He enters his office and tries to close the door to have a bit of privacy so he can pack up his stuff but one of the security men blocks the door. "Sorry Rupert, we need to keep an eye on you packing I'm afraid." Rupert goes to say something but can't even bring himself to protest, he just grabs his bag and starts putting his stuff in it. Laptop, pictures and stationery, he goes to put his notepads in his bag when the security guard who had kept the door open speaks up again. "Sorry Rupert, you can't take your notes, they could contain private information so leave them please."

Rupert is so tempted to throw it across the room in some sort of petulant move but he just puts them back down and finishes packing up his stuff. Once packed he looks back at his office that he had spent so many hours in, and feels a huge emotional heartbreak.

Everyone watches as he is escorted out by the guards and he

sees Stephen stood by his door watching him go and then turn around and head back into his office and shut the door. Once Rupert gets to his car, he puts his stuff in the boot and gets in and suddenly the emotion hits him like a train. He breaks down in uncontrollable sobs.

Chapter 34

Today is a fucking good day! I've just read the press release from Rupert's company. I thought they might suspend him until the investigation had finished but they just went and stuck the knife in. You'll like this part it's my favourite bit "Unfortunately due to circumstances surrounding M. Grahams involvement in the recent criminal investigation we have no choice but to terminate his contract." No until further notice, no until the investigation is over, they went and fired the bastard. I couldn't be happier. I think I might have a little celebration tonight, knowing that he is probably at home right about now getting more and more depressed, hopefully drinking himself to oblivion. That's how he always handles bad news, fucking coward, always using drink to run away from his problems. I hope the fucking press catch him out. That plan worked well didn't it? Releasing his name out into the world. It was so easy just a click of a button and someone can go from a nobody to a somebody. That's what I love about social media just a few messages about someone and you can start an avalanche.

This plan has gone even better than I could have ever imagined. Rupert's life is slowly falling apart bit by bit and I'm just here holding the fucking popcorn enjoying every second. He deserves it for what he fucking did, he hurt everybody in his path so that's what I'm doing to him. When this plan took hold in my brain, I could see it clear as anything. The set up to the murder right through to the fallout was all there in front of me. I've got it all written down, each piece of the plan, to keep me focused and I think I have one last piece to play before you are well and truly fucked Rupert! I can't wait to see that fucking detective's face when she hears what I have arranged, she won't be able to deny that you are responsible. I had hoped not to use this but needs must and if this pushes her towards what should be done, so be it. I mean it's taken them a fucking a week to get their act together. The package should be arriving at any moment. Let's just hope that this works.

Chapter 35

Jess had been called from the meeting because the now daily call from Rupert's ex brother-in-law Jason has come through. The phone call is pretty much the same every day, Jason asking if there has been any more evidence to charge his client. And every day she had the same answer, "Not yet Jason. we are following several leads that are close to finishing but we want to make sure that not stones are left unturned before we bring your client back in, we don't want a repeat of last time if we haven't got anything to present to him in terms of evidence." Today she said pretty much the same thing, she didn't mention the shoe discovery because she wants more digging to be done before she even admits to Jason that they might have got it wrong because for all they know that shoe print was someone who had walked through the alley an hour or two beforehand and it might not even be the killers. They need more time to put all the pieces of the puzzle together, because at the moment it feels like they are completing two different puzzles. During the meeting before she got pulled away by the phone call, she had handed out the updated assignments to the team, John and David were checking out the CCTV of businesses in the area and she had sent Olivia and Isabella off to the shoe shop to find out who had bought those shoes. When she puts the phone down, she's about to head back to the room when she sees them all leaving. Andrew had finished up the meeting for her and he walks over to her office and says, "I told Ava and Jamie to keep going with the background research and to make sure that they reach the ex-wife today. I figured we had covered everything and we can't keep sitting around all day can we."

Jess nods. "Great, thanks Andrew, I'm just going to go and read over some more notes and then do you want to have a meeting?"

Andrew nods but just as Jess is about to enter her office Little Dave comes up to her and says, "Jess someone is in reception for you, they say that they have some evidence for the Graham case." Jess turns to little John "What?"

"Someone wants to give some information against Rupert. They said it's urgent," Little Dave says again.

"Thanks Dave, please go and put them in interview room 1" Jess says struggling to believe it but she runs into her office and grabs her pad and as she leaves walking through the office she shouts "Andrew, I need you." Andrew jumps up and immediately follows as they make their way down the stairs. They get to Interview Room One as Little Dave comes out. "Thanks Dave. Have you got details?"

"Yes, it's a lady named Rose Field. She's thirty-four and wants to give some information on Rupert about an event that happened over fifteen years ago."

"Brilliant thank you very much Dave," Andrew says and with that they enter the room. Jess sees a red headed woman sat opposite the table; she's wearing a nice black coat with a red shirt underneath that looks like it's been recently purchased. Jess also immediately notices she looks nervous; her hands are fidgeting over each other like they are trying to find somewhere to hide but can't settle. "Good morning, Rose, I'm Detective Chief Inspector Jess Spears and this is," she gestures to Andrew, who says, "Detective Inspector Andrew Powell. Pleased to meet you." He holds his hand out to shake hers. "So Rose, what do you want to tell us today?"

She clears her throat and looks at both of them. "I would like to give some information regarding Rupert Graham. I saw his name in the press and watched the recording of the press conference and you said to come forward with any information."

"Thank you for coming forward," Jess says. "Please continue?"

"Rupert and I dated when we were teenagers, this was before he had met his wife, and we had a what was a typical teenage romance. We were each other's umm…"

"Each other's?" Andrew says

She takes a deep breath as though she's about to reveal a big secret. "First, we lost our virginity together. We thought we were in love and we said we would wait and then one afternoon we just went for it."

"How long were you dating?" Jess says, "It was a few months."

"That seems short if you thought you were in love?"

"Well, that was my reason for coming in here, we ended because he started to get a bit weird, he started going on about the new porn that he had watched and he wanted to try it with me," she takes another a breath "He wanted to try BDSM and more importantly he wanted to try strangulation."

Jess and Andrew both look at each other "And what happened?" said Jess Rose looks down and says with a hint of shame. "We tried it and we had talked about it beforehand and said that if we felt unsafe at any time, we had a safe word, so we started and he put his hand around my throat." She stops for a minute, Jess is intently looking at her face just watching as her eyes dart around the room and eventually settles on Jess and continues, "He squeezed and started fucking me harder, I yelled out our safe word but he kept going harder and harder squeezing my throat, I noticed he was smiling he was loving having that power then it all went black." She stops gripping her mouth as though to hold the words back.

"Then what happened, it's okay, it's safe in here," Andrew says.

She continues. "So, I came around after a couple of minutes to find Rupert just sat on the end of the bed, cleaning himself up. When he saw I came around he looked surprised and said 'That was great. Wasn't it such a thrill?' I could see as he said it, he was getting aroused again, he was not concerned about me or the fact that when I looked in the mirror there was…" she pauses and wipes her eyes, "hand marks around my neck, the bruises didn't leave for weeks I had to wear scarfs all the time to just cover them up."

"And that's when you broke up with him?" Jess asks.

"Yes, I was so scared that he might push it further next time. He was obsessed he kept talking about it," she says looking down at her hands which starts rubbing them together again.

"How did he take that?" Jess asks again.

"Not well. He started getting very nasty and said that he would make my life hell. It was just teenage stuff at the time but I definitely saw a side to him that was not nice."

Jess finishes writing her notes and asks the question that is hanging in the room, "Why has it taken you this long to come forward, why did you not come forward back then?"

"Because I was scared of him and I had tried to push it to the back of my mind. It was only when I saw his name in the papers it just brought it all flooding back, and I needed to give my story if it helps get justice for that poor girl. I wish I had said something earlier, I really do," she says looking at Jess.

"I appreciate your bravery for coming forward it can't have been easy."

"I just want to help," Rose replies. "I don't want anyone else getting hurt."

"Thank you, is there anything else you want to add or anything else you can remember?" Andrew asks.

"No, I don't think so I just wanted to make you aware of his fascination of strangulation, just so you were in the know."

"Thank you, if there's nothing else, we will get you to sign a full statement if that's okay," Jess says, she thinks for a split second she sees Rose freeze as Rose says, "Not a problem, as long as it helps."

"Brilliant thank you so much for your time Rose, and thank you for coming in and making us aware of this. It could be a real help to this case. Our colleague, Dave, who showed you in, will come and take the official statement from you."

As Jess gets up, she notices that Rose has what looks like brand-new shoes on, Jess has seen these shoes in the shops and they aren't cheap by any means, she turns back to Rose and asks "By the way, what do you do as a job, Rose?" Looking a bit thrown by the question, Rose answers, "I'm between jobs right now, I was a receptionist at the accountants in town."

"Thank you." And with that, Jess and Andrew leave the room and signal to Dave who's been waiting in the hallway as he approaches the door Jess says, "Please take a full statement from Miss Field, thank you."

As they leave Dave to take the statement, they both make their way back upstairs, as they are walking Andrew says, "Well that's a turn up for the books isn't it, who knew that Rupert would be into that. It just goes to show doesn't it, the people you least expect to be into BDSM are normally the people who love it. It definitely builds a profile about him." Jess who has been deep in thought from the moment they had left Rose in the room turns to him. "Something's not right."

"What do you mean?" Andrew says, as they reach the top of the stairs.

"I don't know but something about the way she told it, and the way she had designer clothes on but no current job. I feel like we have just been played like a fool, something isn't adding up. I'm not saying she is lying but there's something that's not right about it," Jess says.

"Really? I thought it sounded true and her fear seemed genuine," Andrew says.

"Exactly when do you think that fear sounded genuine? Something's not right," Jess says as they enter the office. "Ava?" she shouts across the office.

"Yes, Jess," Ava says looking up from her computer.

"Can you please do a full background check on a Rose Field please, and I mean everything, no stone unturned please?"

"No problem, will get on it now," Ava says immediately returning to her computer.

"Then at least we will be able to find out if she is who she says she is."

"Why do you think she's lying?" Andrew replies, eyeing Jess.

"I can't tell you, just something is not adding up and it feels like something just fell into our laps when we needed it most." She can just feel it in the pit of her stomach and for the first time in this case she suddenly feels not in control of the narrative as if someone is pushing them into a certain direction.

Chapter 36

Who is this calling me? Oh my God it's fucking Rose, what's happened now? I hope that cow has done what I asked. "Hello Ro..." but before I can even get the sentence out of my mouth she has already began "I've done what you asked, but you never said that they would take a full fucking statement! If this doesn't go the way you said it would I could be in serious fucking trouble here!" She sounds frustrated. Rose is one of my friends and when I found out that she had been embezzling her boss's company funds and she confided in me one day thinking I could help, little did she know that I was already planning Rupert's demise and when I heard that information, the idea just came to me. I knew that when I approached her and said either do this or I tell everyone and expose her secret, she had no choice. I told her exactly what to say, I had it all written down I told her when to take a breath and she reluctantly agreed to do it, but it came with a price she wanted £5000 to do it and it was that or no dice. Fortunately, I had just come into some money so I agreed and it worked, she got something out of it and so did I. "Look it's okay, it's routine," I say to her. "Yeah, it is probably routine, but if they find out I'm lying I could be going to prison for perverting the course of justice, you arsehole. This wasn't worth it. Oh, my God I'm going to fucking prison, I knew I shouldn't have done this. I want more money."

"What? We had a deal!" I say down the phone.

"Yeah, well I don't really care If we had a deal what you've just made me do is a fucking criminal offence," she says.

"Don't forget the reason you are in this mess is because you committed a fucking crime in the first place!" I say down the phone, trying not to get angry.

"Well, it's another £5000 now or I turn around and go back into the police station and withdraw my statement and tell the truth, I don't care how much trouble I'm in. This is wrong," she says down the phone.

Ah this fucking bitch! Putting me over a barrel like this. She had one thing to do and now she's freaking out. But I can't afford to let this fail at the final hurdle I knew bringing people in would be a risk but I had to do it.

"Fine, extra five, that's it," I say as I hear her breathe a sigh of relief.

"Fine, but if this goes south, I'm not going fucking down for you!" she says and there's a click and she's gone.

It's fine once all this is over, you won't be going anywhere. Once Rupert is behind bars, I'm going to have to clean up a few loose ends and that means you Rose, I feel like you aren't long for this world anymore. But that's for another time. Thankfully that little bit of information Rose has just delivered to Detective Jess surely will push them in the right direction, it has to!

Chapter 37

John and David are on their way to the street behind the alley way that Jess has sent them to, to look for CCTV. "I can't believe that we are doing more CCTV hunting," David says as he's looking out of the window of the car.

"It's not that bad, David," John says. "I reckon we are closer than you think to finding out what happened that night. CCTV is so important in a case like this! I know its monotonous but let me tell you, that moment where you finally see what happened or something that links someone. There is no feeling like it. I think we will park up here and we will walk down the street." he says as he bumps his car up on the curb. They both get out and the shock of leaving the warm central heated car into the cold winter wind hits them like a ton of bricks. As they walk down the street, they see all the small independent shops who are just trying to survive the winter while tourism is at a bit of a low for the city. They aren't looking in the shops though they are furiously scanning the buildings and the rooftops for any sign of CCTV. They spot one on the hat shop that they had looked at, but they go in anyway and ask if there are any more cameras that face the other way, but unfortunately not.

They are almost at Barber Alley and they are both getting bored "I can't see anything obvious," David says in frustration, John not responding is really staring at all the rooves as they approach the coffee shop. "Oh, my God! How did we miss that?" John says pointing towards the coffee shop roof and David sees poking out of the roof a small white CCTV camera that if you weren't looking for it you would never see. He can't believe they didn't see that and then he remembers that a week ago they were stood outside this coffee shop chatting with the girls. They enter the coffee shop and see the smiley barista that had served Olivia a week ago.

"Hey fellas, how can I help you today?" he says still smiling.

"Hi, I was wondering if you could help us today, we are investigating the murder that happened in Barber Alley last week. I'm sure you have seen it on the news," John says.

"Yes, I've heard it and the two police women came in last week the night after it happened," the barista says.

"Ah great," David says, "So…"

"Jacob." The barista says.

"Jacob, we are looking at all the businesses along the street this end of Barber Alley for any CCTV that might be able to help us in our investigation," David says.

"Well, anything I can do to help, the CCTV system is pretty old though. I got it off Amazon when they were offering the grants."

"That's great," John says, "is it okay if we take a look at it?"

"Yes, not a problem, right though here guys," Jacob says as he points them through to behind the counter. He leads them through a narrow hallway that is filled with disposable cups and coffee beans, to a small office that has one desk in one corner and a monitor in the other. On the monitor you can see the two camera angles that the CCTV system provides; one is the inside of the shop that they were just standing in, and the other the one can see the street that they just walked up – and as clear as day is the entrance to Barber Alley. John who has really no technology experience steps back and says "David, can you see if we can get last Friday's recording off it please?"

David sits down at the monitor and starts trying to go through the menus. Now he's been through many systems of

CCTV over the years but this one was one he had never seen before. As he starts trying to view the footage from Friday, it won't play it back. He starts googling the system on his phone and eventually finds a way to convert it but it's not something he can do at the shop. He turns to John. "This is going to take a while I think, it's a really old system and to be able to view the footage we need to get it converted but it's something that needs to be back at the station." He turns and shouts through to the front "Jacob!" who moments later comes through "Thank you for letting us look at this it's very helpful but we are going to need to take the hard drive I'm afraid because as you said it's quite an old system so we are going to need to convert it back at the station."

"I thought as much, like I said I got off Amazon years ago, but yeah go nuts I just want to help," Jacob says

"Thank you, Jacob, it's so helpful to have someone to who wants to help" John says.

"I'm surprised you guys haven't been here earlier, I mentioned that CCTV last week to that officer who came in," Jacob says.

"Excuse me?" John says.

"Yeah, they came in the day after it happened and I said I wanted to help and said that I had CCTV and the lady said that someone would be in touch. So, I wasn't surprised that you guys came in today!" Jacob says.

John and David looking at each other seem to know what the other is thinking. "Ah yes, we had been told but we've been following other lines of investigation, so this is the first time we have been able to get down here, but thank you for allowing us to take this," John said as David disconnects the system for them to take. As they leave and say their goodbyes to Jacob, they wander back down to their car. They walk in silence; something is bothering them and David is pretty sure that they are both thinking the same thing but can't quite find the words to say it. When they get in the car John is the one to break the silence "If Oliva and Isabella missed the opportunity to get some evidence, they are well and truly fucked!" David nods in agreement, he doesn't know what to say, if they have messed up, he knows that Jess won't stand for it. There's a real possibility that if they had flagged it this case would have potentially have been solved already, they are going to have a wait a few days to know whether Olivia and Isabella truly screwed up.

Chapter 38

Olivia and Isabella are on their way to the shoe shop, they are so pleased about how the meeting went they've been buzzing ever since, even though they don't know that they had potentially missed some crucial CCTV at the coffee shop. As they start to drive through the town Isabella says, "I've heard great things about that place. Do you fancy going there after we've done this, it's Friday after all, we haven't been out since last week."

Olivia turns to Isabella. "Let's see how this goes first, we are probably going to be put on CCTV watch after this so it's not going to be an early finish." Olivia is suddenly reminded of how Isabella is quite a few years younger than her and how new she is to the force. She thinks that Isabella often thinks that this is a 9–5 job but sometimes, and especially in cases like these it's not. She reminds herself that it's not her fault, she's learning.

As they pull into the car park behind the shoe shop, Isabella grabs the evidence pictures as they walk around to the front of ShoeState they can see that it's clearly a brand-new shop. Its front is a recently painted sky blue with the name ShoeState in a dark racing green across the front and across the windows. It's not the biggest shop in the world but once inside the girls see it's stacked to the ceiling with shoes and as they walk down the narrow shop, they see the owner just serving a customer, He's a short mid forty's man who's very smiley. They stand and watch as he serves the customer and the transaction rings through the old till. He says, "Thank you so much, I think you are going to be very happy with these. And if you have any problems with them please come back."

The customer looks up and says, "Will do, thanks for all your help today, Alan."

"No problem," Alan says back to him as he turns and leaves the shop, Alan looks towards Olivia and Isabella and walks out from behind the till.

"Good afternoon and welcome to ShoeState, how can I help you today?" he says with a smile.

"Good afternoon, we aren't actually looking for shoes today. We are with the police, I'm Olivia and that's Isabella," Olivia says as she draws out her badge to show him, his smile disappears and a frown appears on Alan's face, sensing his worry that they are possibly there about the shop Olivia is quick to reassure him. "It's about the murder that happened down at Barber Alley a couple of weeks ago."

Alan still looks confused and responds, "Oh well I'm sorry I don't know anything about that I'm afraid. My house is out of town so I wouldn't have been anywhere near the area." Olivia, feeling slightly exasperated that he thinks he is being interrogated, "No, don't worry that's not why we are here; we are here because we believe that the we have some evidence that has been bought from this shop," she says as the she turns to Isabella. "So, we have this." She indicates to Isabella to bring the box forward. Olivia removes the mould of the shoe that the lab had contracted for them and places it on the counter. Alan says, "Ah I see." He steps forward and looks at the mould "That's definitely one of my shoes." He examines it more closely. "It's our Top Loader shoe. It's new in this year so they have been selling quite a bit."

Olivia is also looking at the mould for anything to jump out and help them narrow this down a bit. "Is there anything that would show any way to narrow down the date they were bought?"

Alan looks up from the mould and says, "Well, I have only been selling these trainers for the past couple of months, so I don't think it would be that hard to narrow down a date."

Isabella jumps in, "It happened about a month ago," she says eagerly. "So that would narrow it down to a month of sales."

Alan smiles. "I would also say that the trainers are new, the heel is hardly worn." He points towards the heel sensing the question from Olivia. "I've been working in the footwear industry all my life and I have fixed many a shoe over the years and you see certain traits of wear and tear on the shoe. These are box fresh. Even if they had been worn for a week there would be scuffing and wear on the heel, it's just the way we walk," he says proudly.

"That's amazing!" Olivia says relieved to hear that they could possibly narrow this down more for that fact that she doesn't want to trawl through hours' worth of paperwork and CCTV.

"Is there any way we could have the records of the sales and CCTV?" she says pointing to the small round camera that's facing them from behind the counter. Alan walks behind the counter and heads towards the door at the back which Olivia presumes leads to a small office.

Moments later he comes back holding a black folder that look like it's bulging with receipts. "Luckily, I have just sorted all my invoices from the last month, so it's all here for you. I'll just grab the CCTV."

"Thank you, Alan, that's so helpful," Isabella adds.

"It's the least I can do. I want to help you," he says as he leaves to go into the back office again.

Olivia quickly flicks through the invoices that Alan has just brought out. She can see the dates, written descriptions of what was bought and the way they paid and she can see a copy of the receipt stapled to the corner. Alan comes back with a USB pen and hands it over to Olivia. "That's got the past three months' worth of CCTV on there. I've just got a new system so it wasn't that hard."

"That's great thanks, Alan," Olivia says as another customer comes in through the door a young mum with two children who are already loose looking at the shoes on the shelves they can reach. "That should be everything."

Alan says, "Do you need me for anything else?"

Olivia says back to him, "No all good, thank you Alan."

"Excellent, I better go and see to those customers before they destroy my entire bottom shelves of shoes," he says, already making his way towards the young family.

Olivia and Isabella grab everything they need and make their way to the exit as they leave and pass Alan, Isabella says to him, "Thanks Alan, we'll be in touch." He gives them a wave as he's in the middle of his sales pitch to the mum. Olivia hears a snippet as she walks past, "Well if you go those shoes you have longevity but if you go with these you really do get a better value for money." She shuts the door to the shop and they leave.

As they get to the car, she puts the file and the USB in a bag in the boot, Isabella says, "He was a bit sketchy, wasn't he? At the beginning do you think he was hiding something?"

"Oh, he's probably got a dodgy shipment of shoes or something. Did you see how many were in that shop? It was ridiculous," Olivia says as she starts the car. "Let's get back to the station. I feel this task is going to take a while. I don't think we will be going anywhere tonight."

Chapter 39

It's been a few days since Rupert got fired from his job. It felt like going through a break up to him. He just couldn't get his head around what had happened. It was like a dream that he had hoped to wake up from. Since the statement from his work had come out, the press had gone into overdrive. The headlines that he had seen had just been on another level "KILLER SUSPECT HAS BEEN KILLED BY PRODUCTION COMPANY," another one read "SUSPECTED STRANGLER PRODUCER CUT BY OWN COMPANY." They weren't even trying to make out he wasn't guilty; they had already decided. He tried to stop reading them, but every time his phone pinged, he couldn't help it. His mum rang him as soon as she found out and reassured him once again that she believed him and all this will blow over. He just ended up sobbing down the phone uncontrollably. He couldn't stop no matter how hard his mum tried to talk him down. Every emotion just came flooding out of him. He could hear that she was trying not to cry down the phone she just kept saying, "I hate hearing you like this, I'm coming down you need someone there." She had done this a couple of times over the last week or so but he always said no and even in the state he was in he said no, he couldn't bear anyone seeing him like this and he didn't want his elderly mum getting wrapped up in press photographs, so he firmly told her no down the phone. Since that phone call with his mum, he's started to ignore the phone, with journalists calling him trying to get a comment from him, he just decides that he doesn't want to speak to anyone. Not that anyone really, apart from the journalists, his mum and Jason have been calling him, all of his friends are keeping their distance form him, he's had no texts of support or calls, they've all turned their back on him since his name has been leaked to the press. He's even noticed lots of people have been blocking him on social media, people he's known for years who have grown up with him are believing that he did this. He did try and reach out to a few friends via text but no reply. He's been left to the wolves and he knows it. Jason has called several times trying to get hold of him but he knows that Jason is not bringing any good news since there's been no further press conference after the eighth call Rupert finally decides to pick up the phone "Hello," Rupert says as his voice cracks from not speaking over the last few days.

"Thank fuck for that, why are you not picking up the phone?" Jason says down the phone.

"Sorry. Just finding it hard to do anything at the moment."

"I know you are, mate, but I am working hard to keep you out of prison so I need you to answer your phone. I know that you don't want hear the news, mate, but I have to tell you to keep you updated. I want you to be aware of what's coming."

Rupert doesn't say anything he just waits knowing that whatever follows is not going to be easy to hear. Jason carries on, "So I have to tell you that someone has come forward to say that you assaulted them in the past."

"What?" Ruppert says after hearing it, he knows it's not true he has never attacked anyone.

"So, they probably won't use it as actual evidence if this ever goes to court but they will use it to create a character profile for the jury, but it's not good news. The police won't release who has said it so I can't find out who they are. Can you think of anyone

151

who would do this?"

"No, no-one. I've never assaulted anyone," Rupert said down the phone hearing the desperation in his own voice.

"Well, someone is saying you have so we are going to have to contest it. When I get the statement, we will be able to work out the dates, but it will most likely become a he-said she-said sort of thing, so we will just have to prove you aren't like that," Jason says.

"Well, we can easily prove it, because it's not true!" Rupert says down the phone.

"Of course, of course and we will Rupert, hang tight and we will get it sorted. I've got to go, I'm just dealing with some other cases while I wait for Jess to come back to me. Keep your head up, mate, it will all get sorted!" Jason says. "Will do, mate," Rupert says, struggling to believe Jason or himself. As Jason puts the phone down. The silence falls over the apartment again. Recently, Rupert finds the silence deafening, he can't stand it so he sticks the TV on even though he's not watching it. The sound settles him. He decides that he needs a drink, it's become an all-too-common thing recently he finds himself reaching for the drink more and more. He's been making his way through whatever he had in the house. As he heads into the kitchen, he opens the cupboard only to find the ring stains that the bottles used to sit on. He starts frantically looking through the other cupboards hoping there's more drink in the house. Once all the cupboards are opened and it's clear his house is dry, the thought is already there and he can't ignore it. He's not ventured outside since he returned home from work, the photographers have only increased since the news of his firing. Fortunately, he has his secret route out the back to his car. He gets his big coat on and a hat to cover his face, as he approaches the door he stops for a minute and feels a pang of anxiety about actually leaving the house, but the need for a drink is more powerful, he knows that if he gets enough, he won't have to leave for a while.

Getting out of the house is easy, he's in the car before he knows it. He pulls out of the garage and slowly turns left away from the photographers and he's free. He puts the radio on to fill the silence that has left him with the thoughts, he's so thankful because the news is just ending and some music comes on, which is a sweet relief. When he arrives at the supermarket, he makes sure that his hat is covering his face and gets out the car and starts heading towards the doors. He feels like everyone's eyes are on him, even though his logical brain is telling him they aren't. Once inside his thoughts turn to getting booze as he grabs a basket and heads straight towards the drink aisle walking past all the papers which have his faced plastered all over them. He doesn't even know what drink he wants, he just knows that anything will do right now. He stands in the aisles and just goes off instinct, he grabs a few bottles of whiskey, vodka and beers. He fills the entire basket up with bottles, much to the disgust of everyone around him, who are all looking and he expects thinking the same thing, that he was a drunk but he would ask anyone what they would do in his situation. Drinking helps numb the pain. He's absolutely positive that some people are recognising him and he's sure he's heard people whispering but he doesn't care he's got what he wanted and he heads for the till. He keeps his hat low so that his face is nearly entirely covered. As he goes through the checkout, the cashier tried to engage in conversation with him.

"How's your day going?"

He replies in a low voice, "Yeah, it's fine thank you."

She puts through all the booze as he packs them in a bag,

when it gets to the end, she says, "I'm going to need some ID please," and she presses a button and signals to the manager. "Sorry, I've not been here that long so I don't have clearance." The manager, a short, angry looking man who seems to be annoyed that he's actually having to do his job, turns to Rupert and asks "ID' in a very gruff tone. Rupert hands it over and the manager takes it and looks at, he pauses for a moment and from under the brim of his hat he sees the manager notice his name and he can feel the judgement. After what feels a like an eternity the manager clicks a button on the till and Rupert see's the total come up. He breathes a sigh of relief and pays. He gets back to his garage without a problem and starts walking towards the back door with the two full bags of booze. As he's walking across the car park, all of sudden five people appear from nowhere, it's the press and they are already taking pictures before Rupert can comprehend what's happening. He starts running towards the door as more paps appear taking photos. He gets in the door and can still hear the clicks of the cameras. He runs up the stairs, the bottles clanging together, not realising that he didn't shut the back door properly. He struggles to get the keys in the lock and fumbles around desperately. He shoves his way in finally and slams the door shut behind him. After a few hours, the stories start to appear online "STRANGLER'S A DRUNK" "MURDERER WAS DRUNK ON THE NIGHT" Rupert just drinks an entire bottle of whiskey to numb his pain and eventually passes out on the sofa.

He's awoken by a hammering on his door, he thinks it's a dream but it's consistent, on and on the banging is going. His eyes focus eventually which helps him get up and stumble towards the door he shouts "GO AWAY" but it keeps hammering, not letting up. He eventually opens the door thinking he was going to find Jason or his mum, but he finds a blonde woman staring at him "Hello" he says in his groggy voice "Can I help you with something?"

She looks at him and says, "I'm Becca! I'm Jennifer's sister."

Chapter 40

Jess is currently sat in her office watching her team out of her window as they scour through hours of CCTV. Her eyes are stinging with tiredness because she's been at the station for at least fifteen hours a day to get to the bottom of this case, she has constantly been checking on her team to see if there are any new updates, to the point she thinks they must be sick of her. When David and John came back with the old CCTV system that was going to take days to decode, she was gutted and she kept asking them if it was ready. This morning there was finally a break through and they said it was going to be ready at about 12 o'clock. It was the same when she saw Olivia and Isabella come back in with the black ring binder full of invoices from the shoe shop. She made sure that they were going through them as fast as possible.

She has also been having constant meetings with Ava and Jamie anytime they have a slight breakthrough with background checks or building a picture of Rupert she has them in and they discuss and decided which ones to go more in depth on and which ones to leave. They still haven't been able to get hold of Rupert's ex-wife, she is definitely dodging their calls, which concerns Jess. She doesn't have to stay as late as she does but she wants her team to know that if they are staying late then so is she.

Something has been niggling at the back of her mind for days now that something in this doesn't add up. The two things that have made her feel on edge are the fact that there was a branded trainer print at the crime scene but Rupert wasn't wearing anything like that when he was brought in. And, Rose Field, the woman who came forward about Rupert being a sexual abuser. It's really bothered her and she has this unwanted feeling that she is being played. She's been wracking her head to try and find a reason and she can't.

Over the past few days, she's been trying to get Rupert in for an interview because she wants to ask him more questions about everything but Jason won't let her anywhere near him. He just keeps saying the same thing over and over again, that until they have proper evidence, they will not be getting his client back in. She knows that they have no leg to stand on since the last interview.

She decides that she can't just sit here and worry about not having enough evidence, she gets up and leaves her office and heads straight for Olivia and Isabella who are busy looking through a pile of paperwork. Jess can see other papers strewn across the desk. It' all go. They haven't stopped since they got back in.

"How's it going team?" Jess say as she approaches their desk. Olivia looks up and says, "I think we have finally gone through every invoice and made a pile of the ones that mention the sale of the Top Loader shoe. How many do we have now Isabella?"

Isabella, who is busy looking through another invoice looks up, "I think we have about one hundred or so sales from the last month."

Already seeing the response in Jess's face, Olivia jumps in, "So we will be splitting these between us when we view the CCTV, so that's only fifty each so it shouldn't take too long. We know the time so can just skip to payments and see immediately who it is."

Jess relieved that they might be able to get the answer from that, "Well done, that is absolutely amazing. Thanks, so much for keeping going over the last few days."

"No worries, it's worth it if we catch someone or at least create a lead, isn't it?"

"Exactly!" Jess says. She walks around the office and starts heading for David and John, who she can see are just waiting for the CCTV to come back from the lab when she is intercepted by Andrew.

"Jess!" he says in a hurried tone, "Can I speak to you in your office please?" Jess makes a hand gesture towards her office and the two of them walk back together, Andrew shuts the door and turns to Jess. "Sorry I didn't want to say it out there, but there is another woman with claims about Rupert saying they had an affair in the early days of his marriage and that he abused her." Jess sits down "What?" Jess's mind is running, this all doesn't make sense, the feeling in her gut comes rushing back up and sits at the back of her throat.

Sensing that they are thinking the same thing Andrew says, "It's all a bit odd isn't it, two people suddenly coming forward making claims, I get one but two, it just seems…"

"Convenient," Jess finishes for him "It's not making sense, I'm starting to get the feeling that someone is making a fool of us. I'm starting to think more and more that Rupert might have been in the wrong place at the wrong time."

"Well, why don't we get Rupert back in?" Andrew asks

"Because the brother-in-law lawyer is stopping us at every turn since Rupert had that fucking panic attack, we haven't got a leg to stand on unless we can get evidence so that's why I have been pushing the team so much."

Andrew just nods. Jess is still sure that he feels guilty about the whole Rupert interview but they have to work with what they have. She has a brain wave and is about to share it with Andrew but holds back, she thinks better of sharing it.

Chapter 41

The kettle clicks off as the low rumble of the water boiling fills the kitchen. Rupert pours the water onto the instant coffee into the two mugs. He needs to wake up from the fog that is currently clouding his mind. The surprise to find Becca at his door hasn't quite sunk in. He's got so many questions. Is she here for revenge or does she want answers? When he opened the door and she introduced herself, he invited her in straight away and made sure she was comfortable on the sofa before asking in a hoarse voice if she wanted a coffee to just bide him some time to think.

Walking back into the lounge he places the coffees on the table and sits down There's an uncomfortable silence between them. Much to Rupert's relief, Becca breaks it. "Thank you for the coffee, you're probably wondering why I'm here."

"I am a little bit to be honest," Rupert says his mind racing at what's going to come next.

"I wanted to come because I've read a lot about you in the press. so, I want to know what happened," Becca says, her eyes begging for him to tell her the truth.

"We had dinner and it went really well and I really liked your sister and I mean *really* liked her. I could see us going on not only a second date but a third and fourth and maybe more. When we left, we had a laugh about setting the next date and I thought I had messed up a bit with trying to touch her a little bit too forwardly, I was nervous, which I know is no excuse but I thought it was going well and someone encouraged me to be that way, but she laughed it off at the end. So, we both had to walk separate ways to go home and I offered to walk her back but she declined which I should have pushed for and it will be the biggest regret of my life. We parted ways and as I was walking down the road towards this flat, I heard a scream cut through the air and I don't know why I just turned and ran back towards the sound, I knew someone was in trouble and I needed to help and that's when I got to Barber Alley and found your sister there. But no one will believe me, they all think I did it because that's how most narratives fit in these cases but I promise I did not do this."

It feels like a bit of a release to say the whole event again knowing that he didn't do anything wrong and there is a bit of anger bubbling that no one believes him. Becca nods taking everything in and finally says, "I believe you, Rupert, I don't think you had anything to do with this, I could tell when I spoke to my sister that night."

Rupert's ears prick. "Sorry you spoke to her that night? What did she say?"

"She said that the date went well and that you were charming and that you had a bit of a disagreement but that she was looking forward to the date." Rupert's heart soared for a second, it makes him feel as though he wasn't crazy for thinking the date went well and secondly, this could clear his name. This is what he's been waiting for!

"You have to go to the police!" Rupert exclaims. "We have to go," he says as he stands up.

"I've already told the police that," Becca says "When they told me about my sister's," she pauses for a moment "death, it was the first thing I told them, but they just dismissed me saying that and I quote, 'You never know who is sitting opposite you.'"

Rupert's elation has just come crashing back down to earth.

If they won't believe someone saying that the date went well then, his last chance of being listened to went out the window.

"There was another reason I wanted to see you today apart from to hear your side of the story and that's because I wanted to hear your voice," Becca continues.

"Why did you want to hear my voice?" Rupert asks.

Becca gets her phone out and hit play and the room is filled with the sound of rustling and a low clicking that sounds like heels walking on a road. Then there is a sudden bang on the phone and a muffle scream, Rupert looks at Becca and she seems to read his thoughts, what fills the room next makes Rupert feel sick. The sound of scuffling and a very muffled man's voice saying, "Quiet, you bitch!" And then it goes quiet and the sound of running footsteps as they disappear into the distance after about thirty seconds the sound of footsteps comes back and another muffled voice which Rupert immediately hears as his own fills the room. "Are you okay? Oh, my God! Oh, my God…" it then clicks silent and with that the room falls into silence. Rupert is trying to process what he's just heard. Becca looks at him from across the room "That's why and that's why I believed you as soon as I heard your voice, I knew you were the second person on that message."

"When… When did you find this?" Rupert says, his voice cracking as a huge wave of emotion comes over him.

"My phone ran out of battery the day I found out that she died and I've been so consumed with grief I didn't want to talk to anyone or hear those condolence messages, I just wanted to ignore it and believe it wasn't happening and then when I finally decided to plug it in I saw her name come up as a missed call and a voicemail and I listened to it. I've listened to it a hundred times and I just knew I need to come and see you and get the truth because the police had already not believed me, I needed proof. If you had sounded like the first voice I would have left and gone straight to the police," Becca says to him.

Rupert's brain is once again firing at a million miles an hour, he wants to run straight to the police station and show them all that they have been wrong this entire time, but he knows that this has to be done right. He gets up and goes to his phone. "What are you doing?" Becca asks.

"I'm calling my ex-brother-in-law, he's my lawyer he needs to hear this and he'll know what to do because we need to do this right," he says to her as the phone is ringing.

"Hi Rupert," Jason says in a tone that Rupert thinks sounds like he was waiting for his call. "Are you okay it's been a few days since I last heard from you?"

"I'm fine, look I need you to come over here, I've got someone here who might be able to help."

"Really, who is it?" Jason asks.

"I can't tell you over the phone. I just need to you come here please. You still have my key, just let yourself in. I think the press are waiting again," Rupert says, full of anticipation.

"Okay, okay I'll be right over. I'm just leaving my office, see you in ten." Jason says and with that he hangs up the phone.

Rupert puts the phone down and goes and sits back opposite Becca. "He will know what to do, he's one of the best lawyers in town. How did you get past the press by the way?"

"Well, I think when you ran from the press last night after they caught you with the booze you left your back door to the building ajar so I snuck in this morning, it was more luck than anything really I didn't want to be spotted by the press. They are taking photos of everyone entering and leaving this building and they were around the front this morning so I just went for it and luckily got in. I closed the door though so no one else can get in," she says. They start chatting about how each of them is doing after Jennifer's death and they agree to sit down and talk after all this has been cleared up just after they have exchanged numbers, there's a loud knock at the door. Rupert gets up and opens the door to find Jason standing there.

"Sorry I came as quicky as I could," Jason said a little out of breath from the sounds of it. Rupert watches Jason's eyes wander past his shoulder to see Becca sat on the sofa. "What's going on?" he asks Rupert.

"Come in and I'll explain everything," Rupert says and lets him in through the door. "This is Becca, she's Jennifer's sister and she has some information," Rupert continues, Becca waves to him from the sofa.

"Hi," she says.

Jason turns to Rupert. "Can I have a word with you please? In private. Sorry, Becca, I just need to talk something through with Rupert."

Jason and Rupert make their way into the kitchen and Jason shuts the door and turns to him "What the fuck is wrong with you?"

Rupert is taken aback. "What do you mean?"

Jason who looks visibly worried says "What do you mean, what do I mean? Why the fucking hell have you got the dead girl's sister, who I might remind you are currently being investigated for potentially murdering, in your fucking flat? I have been working my arse off trying to stop the police calling you back in for an interview and here you are pulling this shit. Sometimes I think you have a screw loose."

Rupert who is starting to think more and more Jason doesn't believe him but knows that out there is evidence that it's not him responds trying not to raise his voice, "There's nothing wrong with me, I didn't invite her over she found me and she has something that I think you will want to listen to."

"If it's about the fact that she spoke to her sister just before she got murdered, I already know that, Jess told me a couple of days after your release, that the sister had said this information but it doesn't clear you Rupert, there's no proof," Jason says.

"No, it's not that there's something else, it's a voicemail." Jason pauses. "You need to hear it. Come on, mate, this might be the answer that we have been looking for to clear my name. That's the goal, isn't it? I got you over here because I figured you would know how to handle it with the police."

Jason who looks a bit more intrigued is silent for a moment and then says, "Fine."

And with that he opens the door and heads back into the lounge. "Hi Becca, sorry about that, what have you got? Rupert says it's a voicemail message." Becca hesitates for a moment and looks at Rupert who nods and with that she gets her phone out and the sound of the message once again fills the flat, once it's finished Jason sits down and is silent. After a few moments he finally speaks. "This is really good, thanks so much, Becca," he says smiling at her.

Rupert's heart once again erupts and the pressure that has been weighing him down falls off him. "We will take this to the police but we need to this to be right, I don't think we will take it right now I need to look at the legal stand point because we need to make sure that we haven't compromised anything by you showing us first before taking it to the police. So, do you mind holding tight and we will all go in the morning? I need to draw up an in-depth statement that makes it iron clad, so there is no way the police can deny the evidence. They are currently doing everything they can to fit Rupert in to the mould of this case. So, we can't have anything that gives them an out, okay?"

Jason says looking at Becca who nods and then turns to Rupert. "Both of you?"

Rupert is feeling frustrated. He just wants to get this done and behind him so he can get back to a normal life reluctantly nods, he understands Jason's reasoning he just wished it didn't have to be this way. "I'm sorry it has to be this way but I don't want them to have anything that they can get out of," Jason says, "but I promise you first thing tomorrow we will be going to the police and we will clear your name Rupert!"

Rupert just nods. Jason grabs Becca's number and they all get up as he and Becca go to leave, he says, "I'll call you both this evening and explain what we are going to do and what time I expect you both at the station. I'll go first and then Becca wait five minutes and then leave, hopefully the press won't suspect anything and don't speak to anyone about this, not even the police until I have this sorted." They both agree and say their goodbyes to Jason. Five minutes later and Rupert is saying goodbye to Becca they hug and he says, "Thank you so much."

Becca replies with, "It's the least I can do, I don't want anyone going down for something they didn't do. I just knew I had to find you and make sure for myself."

"Thank you so much, I'll give you a text later," he says.

"Sounds good, see you tomorrow," she says and heads down the stairs and she's gone. The flat even though the curtains are still shut seems brighter somehow and Rupert for the first time in ages feels like there is hope on the horizon.

Chapter 42

Jess and Andrew have been discussing what to do with the woman who's waiting downstairs. The idea has been building in her head and she's decided to go and speak to Rupert alone "Right, well we need to find out what this woman has to say, even if it just helps us build a background report on Rupert, just in case we ever need it."

Andrew looks at her with a quizzical look. "Even though she might be lying?"

"Yes, even so because if someone is messing with us then we need evidence for that as well. Do you mind just taking it?"

"Do you not want to do it together?" Andrew asks.

"No, I'm sorry I need to go and sort something else," Jess says "I'm sorry, Andrew. I don't want to leave you in the lurch but just take her details and get a statement and we will keep it in our back pocket."

Andrew looks as though he is about to argue it and then thinks better of it and eventually says, "Yeah no problem I'll get that done right now, is there anything else you need?"

"Can you send Little Dave in please?" she says to him.

"No problem," and with that Andrew leaves the room and she sees him head straight to Little Dave and he gets up and heads towards her office and knocks on her door.

"Come in," Jess says.

"Hi ma—" He catches himself. "Jess, Andrew said, "you wanted to see me."

"Yes, can you do me a favour, but can you do it on the quiet, I don't want to the team to know what's happening, is that understood?"

Little Dave who although he looks slightly confused nods and says, "Yes that's fine Jess, whatever you want me to do." Sighing a relief, she says, "I want you to call a press conference for about two hours' time, okay?"

"Yes, that's fine, have we had a break in the case?" Little Dave asks.

"No not yet, but I'm hoping to find something today. If they ask what it is about just say that we have made progress in the case and we want to update them."

He writes it all down on his note pad. "That's no problem."

"Amazing, thanks David and remember to keep it on the QT"

"Will do." And with that Little Dave leaves.

A little while later Jess has packed all of her notes up and gathered what she thinks she needs to question Rupert. She knows this is risky and that it could possibly destroy the entire case but she can't ignore this feeling and she needs answers and this is the only way she can get it. She leaves her office and as she walks past the team, she stops between them and says "Hi guys, I'm just popping out for a couple of hours to have a different view to read over these case note. I am available on my phone and if anything comes in do not and I repeat do not hesitate to call me. No information is too small."

There's a resounding mumble of agreement from the office and Jess heads out, passing Andrew on the way down the stairs he asks here where she going. She gives him the same reason about needing a change of scene to which he looks like he doesn't believe but eventually just says "Well, you need to get out, you've been sat in the office far too long, it's enough to make anyone go stir crazy. Give me a call if you need anything. I'm just going to write up the statement from that woman. I'll ping it over to you when it's done and let you decide how we proceed." And with that they say their goodbyes and carry on their separate ways as Jess gets in the car, she's full of worry whether she is doing the right thing but she knows that this has to be done. It's the only way.

Chapter 43

I really don't fucking understanding what the police are doing. I've left them a breadcrumb trail which even an idiot could have followed to Rupert. I've been sat here for a few days just waiting for the article or the press release to say that they had arrested Rupert on a murder charge, even thinking about that now brings a smile to my face. I know I shouldn't have sent the second girl today but needs must. I just wanted to help them build a nice solid background on Rupert to help them see what the monster that he really is.

This is so frustrating this has been months and months of planning and it's all falling down because of the police's ineptitude. Just my luck that I ended up with the shittest police force in the country. I've given them everything they needed and more and they still are dragging their heels. This is just not happening fast enough I want him behind bars now so I can gloat and celebrate that the world is a better place. I'm a very impatient person, once I have set my mind to something that's that I want it done, no matter what.

The longer this goes on the greater the chance that they might start listening to Rupert and when that happens its fucking game over! I feel like I'm running out of options here, this can't have been all for nothing, I can't let that happen, no sorry I won't let that happen! BANG! There goes my mug across the room, I can't help it. The anger and frustration are just building. It feels good. A release from all the pain that I have been put through with that bastard. *BANG! There goes the keyboard. God that felt good. I don't care, I'll just get another one. I need to get this anger out! It's eating me up inside that he is still walking free. BANG! There goes the desk this time it's just a cheap Ikea desk but my God I need that. Need that release! The room looks a right mess but I feel alive. Ah I'm such an idiot! I'm not out of options yet I still have one last one, which was my original plan before I came up with this one. Rupert has to die, it's the only way. He has to pay for what he's done when I started this, I thought this was going to be more satisfying but it's just becoming more and more frustrating and if the police aren't going to do it for me, I'm going to have to do it myself... I don't know if it's the adrenaline or the anger but I can't let him get away with this anymore. He has to pay for what he has done; he has caused too much hurt for him to walk away from this scot free.*

I'm getting in the car when DING DING another fucking text message. I'm not even going to look at this one, I don't want to be distracted by anything so away the phone goes. This needs to be done. Rupert needs to fucking die!

Chapter 44

Rupert has been so optimistic since Becca visited him, his world feels a lot brighter and although he is feeling better, he's feeling impatient at getting tomorrow out of the way. He's got an image in his head of how it's going to go, the relief as he sees Jess and her team's face drop when they hear that it's not him. He knows that Jason is going to take them to the cleaners once this is done, and Rupert knows they won't have a leg to stand on.

He's so happy that Becca came and found him and just showed some faith in him to bring the evidence and she was so nice and the fact that all she wants is the truth. He needs her in his corner. He texts her a couple of hours after she left to make sure she was okay and he's not heard back but from her. He feels that there is this unspoken connection between them because this tragedy has united them and he knows that she wants what he wants, which is justice for Jennifer and for this to be over once and for all.

To keep himself busy he's decided to clean the house and get himself sorted, he opens the curtains and lets light in the flat. For the first time in days he can see the mess that he's created and is ashamed of himself. It takes him about an hour or so to clean and he's found it cathartic and it's done its job. It's distracted him. Once he's finished tidying and stacking the dishwasher, he decides he needs to call his mum. He knows that Jason said not to talk to anyone but he knows that his mum is sat at her house worrying about him. "Hi mum," Rupert said with a cheery tone.

"Rupert, thank goodness I've been calling you and you've not answered and then I saw that story about you and the booze I was this close to getting the car," she said down the phone with a hint of anger.

"I'm sorry, Mum, I should have called, I've not been dealing with this well but I have some news," Rupert said.

"Oh no, Rupert what's happened now?" she says.

"Nothing bad, mum, I promise, It's good news. So, the sister of the girl came and found me today, I know that sounds a bit crazy, I'm aware of that," Rupert says, he waits for a response but his mum is silent on the phone. He's sure she's thinking of a number of terrible scenarios in her head he carries on. "She came today and had some evidence that puts me in the clear, it's a pocket dial voicemail and you can hear the killer and then you hear me approach." Just saying it out loud feels like this is really happening. He waits for his mum's response and hears a sharp intake of breath; his mum is crying. "Mum?" he asks again.

"Yes," she says in an emotional voice. "I'm sorry, these are happy tears, I'm just so relieved, and I'm so happy that this is nearly over," she carries on.

"I know, Mum, I can't believe it either. I'm not meant to say anything but I wanted you to know so you're not worrying. Jason and I are heading to the station tomorrow and then it will hopefully all be cleared up."

"I'm sure it will son, that is such good news," she says.

"Thanks, Mu..." The door buzzer goes; he decides to ignore it. "Thanks Mum, it's such a relief, I can't te..." The door buzzer goes again. "I'm sorry, Mum, someone's at the door I'm going to have to go."

As he starts to approach his front door the door his mum

says, "Okay, no worries, be safe, give me a call afterwards please."

"Of course, Mum. Bye, Mum, love you."

"Bye, love you," his mum replies.

He tentatively presses the button, not sure who it could possibly be and says, "Hello?" through the intercom system the voice that comes back to him is not one he was expecting, "Hi Rupert, it's Jess."

Chapter 45

Jess arrives at Rupert's flat glad to see that nearly all of the press has left thanks to Little Dave's press conference call, she can see one or two photographers still hanging about but nothing compared to the what she has seen outside this flat over the last few weeks. She looks around her car for anything that could possibly cover her face and is grateful when she sees the beanie hat that she had worn recently on a walk with Joseph when they had been walking for the day in the south downs. That trip feels such a long time ago, she makes a mental note to herself that once this is over, she will take him away for a long weekend and just spend quality time with each other and laugh and forget about the world of crime that seems to be dominating their lives at the moment. She had to stop and get a coffee on the way over to Rupert's because she thought she was going to fall asleep at the wheel, her eyes desperately trying to close themselves for the relief of sleep. As she parks up and gets out the car, she's shocked by the cold winds that seem to have a grip on the city at the moment. She puts the beanie hat on and heads towards Rupert's building. As she's walking towards it, she is running through the list of questions she has for Rupert and trying to figure out the right wording to not spook him.

As she gets towards the door, she presses the buzzer. She gets no response. She waits, praying that the two photographers who are milling about don't suddenly get interested. She presses the button again and when Rupert answers, there is silence after she said it was her "Look Rupert I just want to talk, can you let me in please?" After what seems like an eternity the door clicks and Jess is in. When she arrives at the top of the stairs the door is open and Rupert is waiting for her and gestures for her to come into the flat.

"Thank you, Rupert, for letting me in," Jess says, "I just wanted to come and talk to you, one to one."

"So, you can get a confession out of me," Rupert says clearly rattled by the fact that she is here. She had already thought that he might act like this when she arrived.

"No of course not, Rupert, this is strictly off the record whatever is said here can not affect the case. I just have a couple of question to confirm a few things."

He gestures towards the sofa where Becca had sat a few hours ago. Once Jess has sat down Rupert says, "I don't know, Detective, I think I should call Jason. I don't think I should be talking to you."

"Look, Rupert, I'm taking a massive risk by being here. I'm here because something is not feeling right about this case, it feels as though some things are happening and the people coming forward just don't seem to fit with the person I saw in that interview. I just need answers and to be honest I'm sick of being blocked and want to talk to you, person to person, not detective to suspect, does that make sense?" She watches Rupert process it and then he slowly nods.

"Okay great, so my first question is do you know someone called Rose Field?"

Rupert looks at her in a confused look. "No, I don't, why?"

"Well because she has come forward saying you were into BDSM and had a fascination with strangulation."

"What?" Rupert says, "That's rubbish, I don't know anyone

175

called Rose Field and I am certainly not into any of that."

"That's what I thought," Jess says. "It really hasn't sat well with me because the person who I met on the day of your arrest didn't seem like the sort to be into that, not saying you can't be but after years of profiling people I can tell you aren't the type."

Rupert just sits looking worried on the sofa, Jess carries on so the room doesn't stay silent too long. "You see to me it feels like someone might be just setting you up and trying to manipulate the case to put you in a light that can easily be used in court as a profile. It's a classic case of he said she said, but I needed to see you to answer it because I believe you, Rupert, I don't think that you have done this and I'm so sorry it's taking me this long to say it, but I had to be sure I couldn't just write you off straight away."

She sees relief in his face that's all she wanted to see from this meeting and confirm her suspicions. "Do you have any idea…"

Before she can finish Rupert interrupts her, "I have some information to give to you," he says. Jess intrigued, gestures for him to carry on. "Jenifer's sister came to see me today, I really shouldn't be telling you this. Jason said not to say anything but this is firmly off the record, isn't it?"

"Of course, it is, I'm not even meant to be here so even if I was to go back to the station with this information, I can't use it until we gather it ourselves. Please carry on," Jess replies.

"She came by today because she had finally turned her phone on yesterday since you informed her about her sister's death and there is a voicemail on it that is a pocket dial and it shows me arriving after she's been killed; Jason is just making sure it's iron tight before we come down to the station tomorrow and hand it in." Jess takes it all in and just sits there thinking, she can't believe the feeling that she had been right. She can't find the words after a few minutes of both of them just sat in silence waiting for someone to break the silence Jess finally speaks, "Oh my god, can I hear it?" is all she can say.

"Becca's got the only copy which she is bringing to the police station tomorrow morning," Rupert says.

"Rupert, that's brilliant! That would be enough, if we can voice match you then we can rule you out entirely. I also have to tell you that we are currently going through two different CCTV sources which I think will identify the killer. I'm hoping to hear about that today. I don't want that information going anywhere, not even to Jason. You've trusted me with that information now I'm putting that trust in you," Jess says to Rupert who nods and says, "Absolutely."

"If this is a set-up, do you have any idea who might be doing this to you Rupert?" Jess asks.

Thinking about it for a few moments Rupert says, "I don't know, I mean the only bad relationship I've had over the past year has been with my ex-wife but she has moved north as far as I'm aware and she got what she wanted she ended up with half of everything."

"Yeah, we've been trying to get hold of her but she has proven quite elusive, so do you think she has anything to with this?" Jess says

"She's working on a project at the moment so maybe that's why you can't get hold of her," he says. "Plus, the voice in that voicemail is a man's voice, so it wouldn't have been her."

"She could have hired someone potentially, you never know, just something to think about, but as I say we will know by the end of today, well hopefully in the next hour or so we will be able to see who it is."

Rupert, who's deep in thought over what she just said, is clearly thinking that hadn't dawned on him that someone close to him could have possibly been messing with him this entire time.

"This will end, Rupert; don't worry we will get to the bottom of this and your name will be cleared," she says trying to reassure him as she sees his face sink slightly and a tear appear in the corner of his eye.

"Thank you, Jess, you have no idea how much that means to me, that's all I wanted is for someone to believe me and I've now heard it twice today. It's just a lot of emotion," Rupert says in a tearful voice.

She gets up and gives him a hug and says, "It's going to be okay. Now I'm going to have to go because they will notice that I've been gone from the station a long time and I don't want to jeopardise this case by me being here and Rupert all of this has been off the record, I know I've said it a few times but I really just need to hammer home that point," Jess says.

"Yes of course, I won't I promise. I just want this to be over," Rupert says.

With that Jess gets up and heads towards the door as she opens it, she turns and gets out her card and hands it to Rupert "If you need me any time, call me." Rupert takes the card and places it on a little table by the door where he keeps his keys and random pieces of post "Of course, I will," he says.

"See you tomorrow," Jess says.

"See you tomorrow," Rupert says with smile.

Chapter 46

The drive over here wasn't terrible at all, pretty good traffic for the afternoon. Not that I noticed I was too busy thinking about what I was coming here to do and that feeling of satisfaction when the world is rid of that bastard and I never have to hear the name Rupert Graham ever again. The way I've played this I reckon his funeral will be a lonely place. Just the thought of that is making me smile, not like a wry smile where only the corner of your mouth turns up, I'm talking a big smile, a fucking toothy grin.

Almost there. Parked the car a few minutes away so I'm walking on foot, the gun is tucked in the waistband of my jeans. I can feel the cold metal grazing my leg every now and then as I'm walking. I'm trying to think about whether I just shoot him straight away or wait and drag it out so I get the feeling of glee as I watch him slowly work out that it was me all along and then when he's on his knees and I see the acceptance that he has brought this on himself. Yeah, I'm definitely going for B. I want to see it for myself and for him to know everything and then see my face as the last face he sees. I'm also going to make it look like a suicide so it has no trace back to me. Ah nearly there, not too long now!

Shit! Shit! Shit! What the fuck is she doing her, that fucking police chief has just walked out of the flat! Shit! Shit! Shit! I can't believe it. Why is that bitch trying to stop me and every fucking turn. How can I make it look like a suicide now if she's just spoken to him, for fuck sake? Ahhhh I'm so fuming, think! think! think! There's got to be a way around it. Fuck it. I'm going to do it; it needs to be done the world has to be rid of Rupert. Thankfully that bitch didn't shut the front door properly so in I go. Ah my heart is pumping as I'm climbing the stairs. This is it. Knock! Knock! Knock!

Chapter 47

Rupert is just making a cup of tea thinking about the conversation he had with Jess, he knows he wasn't meant to say anything but it just felt right. He of course is not going to tell Jason any of this and he knows that Jess wouldn't either because she came here off the record. It felt such a relief to tell her and to hear that she believed him. It finally feels like this is all coming to an end and he can get on with his life. After this he's thinking he might take a long holiday somewhere nice and warm and get away from here for a little bit clear his head. He still hasn't heard from Becca but he will give her a call later on to check she is okay. Walking back into the living room he's just about to sit down when there's another knock on the door. Rupert is a bit startled by the fact that the door has gone again. He wonders if it is Jess coming back to confirm some more information. He walks over to the door trying to prepare himself in case it is Jess again and opens the door.

Chapter 48

Around the same time that Rupert is receiving a knock on the door, John, David, Isabella and Olivia are all trawling through CCTV. The coffee shop CCTV finally came through about twenty minutes after Jess had left. The had all thought it was a bit odd, her sudden exit from the building. John was convinced that she had found a lead and was checking it out before bringing it to the team. He's known Jess for a long time and knows she likes to play her cards close to her chest. The others shut him down almost instantly saying that she would have said something, but he's sure she has found something.

David and John having been going through the CCTV for about half an hour, speeding through it until they get closer to the scene of the crime. Olivia and Isabella are working their way through customers of the shoe shop, they each have taken a set of receipts and bring up the individual's face running it through their face recognition system and putting together a pile of potential suspects. So far, they haven't found very many, it's mainly families with young children who don't have any record. Olivia is convinced that they will find something soon though because she's sure that this is a key piece of evidence, she can feel it.

"How are you getting on?" Olivia asks Isabella.

"Fine, just so many people buying these shoes," she replies.

"Yeah, tell me about it. But we must be close, someone is bound to show up," she says hoping that's true.

After a few more clips with nothing to show she gets up and makes a coffee to give her eyes a break, she sits back down and hits the next clip. The date flashes up in the corner. It's two days before the murder and as she watches while sipping her coffee, the individual that approaches the till, is instantly recognisable to her. She watches as they pay, smile and say their goodbyes as they leave the shop. She puts her coffee down and tries to comprehend what she has just watched and just in case her eyes aren't playing tricks on her. "Isabella!" she says.

"Yeah." Comes from behind the computer screen opposite her.

"Do you mind running your eyes over this? I think I've found something." As Isabella gets up and wanders over, they watch the clip again. On the other side of the room David and John have also just reached the time of the murder, they are watching together David looking at the detail and John sat back a little to see if he can spot anything across the whole picture, as the clock turns to 22.45 a minute before the murder they see a figure appear in the bottom right-hand corner start to walk towards the entrance of the alley way. Their head is to the back of shot and as the clock ticks closer to 22.46, the figure suddenly turns to look down where they have come from. "There!" John shouts, startling David who instinctively hit pause. "Click back two seconds." David taps back two seconds, they both look at one another.

Olivia and Isabella who are also sat in silence at the individual they have just watched again for a third time to really make sure. "Everyone, we've found something!" David shouts across.

"So, have we!" Olivia replies as they run over to David's desk as they all crowd round and look at the face of the individual on pause. Olivia breaks the silence "Same person on our CCTV."

John immediately gets up and goes to Andrew who's in the meeting room, he knocks on the door... "Andrew! We need to call Jess right now."

Chapter 49

Jess is speeding down the road to get back to the station, lost in her thoughts thinking about Rupert and what he had just said to her. Her phone starts ringing – Andrew's name is flashing up, she answers.

"Hi Andrew, any news?"

"Jess, we have them," he replies in an excited voice.

"What?" she says.

"We have them. We have a match on both CCTV, we've dispatched officer to their home, just sending the image through to you now."

Jess immediately pulls over and grabs her phone from the passenger seat and sees the notification from Andrew, she opens the phone and sees the person before her. She is lost for words.

Chapter 50

Rupert standing at the doorway says, "Hello, come in, come in" gesturing Jason in through the door. "What are you doing here? I thought we weren't meeting until tomorrow morning?"

"I just thought I would drop by and make sure everything was good with you after earlier?" Jason says.

"Ah yeah, I'm fine, mate. Happy that it's all going to be over. Take a seat mate. Tea? Coffee?"

"Coffee, please," he replies.

Rupert heads off and sticks the kettle on and as it starts boiling Jason appears at the door. "Did you believe her earlier? Becca?"

"Yeah, I did, I don't know why she would lie about it and especially come here. It's too risky, so yeah I've not heard from her though so I hope she shows up tomorrow."

"I'm sure she will," Jason says as he walks back into the living room.

The kettle clicks off and Rupert pours the coffee into the cafetiere and just waits for it to brew for a moment. As he's waiting, he gets his phone out of his pocket and sees no new messages. He thought Becca would have at least text him back by now. He dials her number and as he hears the first ring he shouts through to Jason. "I'm just going to call her." As the phone rings, he hears a vibrating sound coming from the lounge. He thinks he must have misheard it, but as the phone keeps ringing, the vibrating still comes from the other room. He walks towards the living room and finds Jason standing by the sofa, holding a phone that's vibrating. Rupert looks at Jason and then to the phone, he thinks he can see his name flashing up on the screen but he must be wrong. He ends the call and with that the phone lays still and the screen goes black in Jason's hand.

Rupert breaks the silence. "Is that Becca's phone?"

Jason doesn't respond. He just looks at the phone and calmly puts it down on the table.

Rupert asks again, "Is that Becca's phone?"

Jason just looks at him. "It was supposed to be so easy."

"What?" Rupert says, clearly confused.

"It was supposed to be so easy; you were supposed to be the prime suspect and deny it but the evidence would be right there so you would have no choice but to plead guilty, but you couldn't even do that right could you? You had to have a fucking panic attack and fuck everything up, didn't you?" Jason says in low but steady voice.

"What are you talking about?" he asks, struggling to understand what Jason is saying. It doesn't make any sense. Rupert's first thought was that Jason was drunk but the words weren't slurring.

"You're such an idiot, Rupert, I really didn't want it to come to this! But you've given me no choice. Why couldn't you just accept your fate?" he says through gritted teeth.

It clicks in Rupert's head, Jess's words coming back to him. "It's you! You've been doing this to me!"

"Yes, of course I have," Jason says with a smirk as if he's proud of it. Rupert is appalled.

"What!? I don't understand, why would you do this to me?"

"Why?" Jason says with anger in his voice "Why wouldn't I do this to you, you bastard. You broke my sister's heart!" Jason

187

moves forward slowly towards Rupert who's not sure what he is talking about it.

"What do you mean?" he asks.

"Don't act like you don't know what I'm talking about. I know exactly what happened between you and my sister!"

"I have no idea what you're talking about," Rupert says.

"STOP SAYING THAT," Jason shouts making Rupert jump. "I know how you treated her." Before Rupert can say anything, he starts again. "She told me everything, you know. I know you thought she didn't, I'm sure you thought that she would disappear in the shadows but she didn't, she came and told me and my family everything about what you did, and that's when I started planning on how to take you down and make sure your life was ruined forever!"

"What have I done to her? She cheated…" Rupert starts before he is interrupted by Jason. "Don't you dare say those lies again, I know that you cheated on her multiple times and that you were abusive to her. She was lucky to get out alive by all accounts. Can you imagine the guilt I felt that I introduced you to her? God it made me feel sick! I was so angry and then when you asked if we could still be friends and act like it didn't happen, that's when my plan formed, I realised that people like you, Rupert, never learn, and that you needed to pay for what you had done!" Rupert's mind is spinning someone who he had trusted had been working to set him up all this time, his oldest friend as well. He has no words but it doesn't matter anyway because Jason carries on regardless. "Do you know that I came to kill you about three months ago? I sat outside this flat and was ready to do it. It was the only way I could see to make the world a better place." He spits the next set of words out of his mouth with such anger. "You had to not be in it!" Jason starts pacing side to side.

"You see that's when I start thinking, Rupert, you don't deserve to die because that's too easy for someone like you! An abuser! I tried to convince my sister to report you and she wouldn't, she was too scared. So, I had to do something that made sure you went to prison so I could sit and watch you suffer! Then what do you do? You come and tell me you have a date for next Friday. You actually told me! I just thought you had a fucking nerve after what you had done to my sister!"

Rupert goes to talk, "Jason I don't what she has said but it's not t—"

"SHUT UP!" Jason shouts.

"She's lying," Rupert says.

"SHE'S NOT LYING, YOU'RE THE FUCKING LIAR HERE," he shouts. He stares at Rupert. "You see when I killed that girl, it felt amazing. It really did, because I knew it meant the end of you. And then it got even fucking better when you actually called me to represent you, the golden opportunity to watch it all happen right in front of me!" he says with glee. "But it made feel sick when you made up that terrible lie about my sister cheating on you. I was so angry I thought I would kill you right then and there."

"But that's the truth!" Rupert says in a plea of desperation; his brain is trying to work out how to get help. He can't use his phone because he can't get it at angle to see the screen to put the passcode in, and if he tried to raise it, he would alert Jason. "She did cheat on me! She broke my heart. What she's told you is to save face so you don't think badly of her," he says, "You have to believe me! You've been lied to!"

"NO, I HAVEN'T," he shouts at Rupert. "You are the liar here, why couldn't you just accept your fucking fate and go to jail? When you had that panic attack, I knew I had to step up the game so I tried everything to force the police's hand to charge you. I tipped off the press while we were waiting in the doctor's office, I sent two women to give evidence against you for sexual assault and abuse to give them a huge advantage in your case. I even blackmailed the waitress at the restaurant to make it out like you were trying to touch the woman up all the time, I wasn't going to ever fight them as soon as they charged you, I was going to do the bare minimum to make sure you ended up in jail for life! But you ruined that, I even tried to force you to work to get you to make sure you got suspended, just to make sure you lost everything!"

Rupert can't believe what he is hearing, someone he had trusted since he was young has been doing this to make sure he went to prison for something he didn't even do. He doesn't know what to say, he's gutted and a sudden rush of anger comes to the surface. "You have ruined everything for me, over a fucking lie," he says to Jason.

"There you go again spouting that it's a lie, you are like a broken record Rupert, that's why you don't deserve to be on this planet anymore. People like you need to be got rid of."

"And you've given yourself the power to do that, have you? You're not God, Jason!" Rupert says to him standing his ground, the anger is rising more and more he can't believe that Jason has done this to him.

"When you have hurt my sister the way you have, then yes, I am," he says.

"She is lying to you, I don't know how many times I have to say this until you believe me, but she is lying to you. She had an affair when she was away with the executive producer, his name is Martin Johnson, she admitted it all, she told me. I found the messages and confronted her and she admitted it! *She* left *me*

Jason, not the other way around, she made a choice to have that affair!" Rupert said.

"It doesn't matter how many times I saw the bruises and the hurt that's all the proof I needed" he says getting slightly quieter.

"What do you mean bruises?" Rupert asks.

"The bruises on the top of her arms, when she told me about it, I asked to see them and when she had the courage, she eventually showed me them and how the fuck could you do that to my sister? She's the best thing to happen to you and you fucked her over and abused her."

"I didn't do that to her! She must have done that herself," Rupert says.

Jason stops pacing and stares at him and makes a move forward. "Don't you dare say that my sister did that to herself when you did it, just to try and save yourself. It's fucking despicable, you betrayed us both, Rupert," he says.

Rupert's anger is starting to hit the point of no return

"I did not do it! She has fucking lied to you," he says and then has a brainwave. "But it's too late for you now, now that there's evidence of me not doing it! Becca's ruined your plan," he says to Jason.

"Why do you think I am here?" he says as he pulls a gun out from his coat, and points it straight at Rupert who immediately backs up and hits the door frame of the kitchen. Jason starts walking towards Rupert. "Do you know how much my heart sank when you called me over to show me evidence that you didn't do it? I knew I had to do something. First thing was to make that fucking sister disappear."

"What have you done with her?" Rupert says as he tries to back further into the kitchen so he could use his phone out of Jason's eyeline.

"Nothing yet, she's currently tied up in my shed, drugged up, but don't worry she won't suffer. She won't go the way her sister went. Plus, the evidence is gone. I deleted the message the moment I got my hands on that phone." Rupert's heart sinks, the evidence that clears him has gone. Jason takes a step further forward, which pushes Rupert further into the kitchen, Rupert knows there is no way he can use his phone because Jason can now see.

"Please don't hurt her she's done nothing to you," Rupert pleads hoping to appeal to Jason's rational side. "Come on you don't want to do this."

"It's too late," Jason says, "You have to die for what you have done, Rupert. It's the only way now that my plan has..." he pauses and then says with anger "failed." He steps closer and closer to Rupert who steps back and back until he hits the kitchen worktop. Jason who can see he's trapped walks even closer to him and in a few steps he's in arm's reach of Rupert. Rupert lifts his hands to stop Jason coming any closer but Jason in one swift move, gets the gun under Rupert's chin.

"Now, now Rupert, don't do anything stupid," he says as he grabs one of Rupert's arms and holds it down. "I can't wait to do that press conferences, expressing how sad I am that you felt this was your only way out and how the police handling of your case drove you to despair. You see, I get two birds with one stone this way. Whenever I have a case with the police of this city, they will be so scared of the outcome they will just let me do what I want." As he finishes the sentence, a wide smile comes across his face. Rupert with a feeling of despair, a million thoughts running through his head, the one that is making the most noise is that this is it, he's going to die at the hands of his best friend over a lie, his heart rate flies through the roof. "Please, please don't do this. It's a lie, it's all a lie." Jason pushes the gun further into his chin the cold end of the barrel cutting into his skin. "IT'S ALL A LIE," Rupert shouts, "SHE WOULDN'T WANT YOU TO DO THIS IF SHE KNEW WHAT IT HAD STARTED, PLEASE DON'T DO THIS. PLEASE, PLEASE, PLEASE.'

"It's too late, dear Rupert, it has to be done. You have to pay for what you have done and I tried one way and it failed, so there is only one option left," he says calmly not listening to Rupert at all. Rupert is just about to shut his eyes to prepare for the worse when out the corner of his eye he sees his knife block, he reckons he can get his free hand around it.

"Okay, okay I will tell you the truth," he says hoping to buy some time so he can slowly move his hand.

"Go on," Jason says taking the pressure off Rupert's chin a little.

"I'm not lying when I say that she cheated on me but I did cheat on her a few times," he lies. "It was a huge mistake and I'm sorry for causing all the upset to your family and I didn't mean to betray you."

Jason smiles and replies, "That's all I wanted to hear, I wanted to hear you say it before you die and know that you caused this. It's your own fault. I always knew you would see sen…" Rupert grabs the knife block and in one swift move brings it into contact with Jason's temple. The knives fly out all over the floor. Jason stumbles back holding his head and Rupert takes the opportunity to hit him again with the knife block and this time strikes the arm that is holding the gun. Jason screams out in pain and drops the gun. Rupert kicks it away. He stands above him holding the knife block ready to hit him again if he gets up. "Stay down," Rupert says as he tries to get his phone out of pocket and starts dialling 999. As he hits in the second 9, Jason swipes his feet taking out Rupert's legs. Rupert is on the floor; the phone goes skidding away across the kitchen tiles and within an instant Jason is on top of him. He overpowers him and grabs the knife block out his hands. He goes to bring it down on Rupert's head. Rupert brings his hands up to stop him and feels the pain course through his arm. "Just fucking die, you bastard!" Jason is screaming at him and goes to bring the knife block down again. Pain courses through Rupert's arm as the knife block makes contact again. He feels his forearm break with the force that Jason his putting through it and screams out in pain. "JUST DIE!" Jason screams at him, then smashes the knife block down for a third time. Rupert, pushing through the instinct not to hold up the broken arm put them up again and this time manages to grab the block as they wrestle with it; Rupert is screaming as he uses all of his might and manages to rip the knife block out of Jason's hand. Jason loses it and starts to use his hands to try and hit Rupert in the face. He stills holds his arms up and manage to hold Jason's arms at bay.

"Why won't you just die!" Jason screams with anger at Rupert who's using all of his strength to hold him back. He can feel his arms wavering as the pain becomes too much. His arms begin to buckle and he sees Jason quickly look to his left and then pushes with all of his strength down on Rupert with one hand aiming for his throat. Rupert feels like he is holding him off then he sees Jason smile and a searing pain comes flooding through his body. Rupert looks down, he can see one of his kitchen knives protruding from his stomach and then with a big grin on his face Jason pulls the knife out. Rupert screams in pain. Jason grabs him by the throat and forces him to look him straight in the eye and says, "I want my face to be the last face you see." Rupert is screaming out in pain and neither of them hears the sudden bang from the other room. Jason's looking at Rupert watching him and smiling. Then bang. Jason suddenly crumples off Rupert and above him holding the knife block is Jess she drops to her knees and sees the blood on Rupert's T-shirt.

"Oh shit. It's okay, it's okay you are going to be fine," she says as she grabs a tea towel from the oven door and puts pressure on Rupert's wound. With the other hand she gets her phone out and rings 999. "This is Detective Chief Inspector Jess Spears; I need ambulance and police back-up. There has been a stabbing. Please hurry." With that she puts the phone down. "It's going to be okay Rupert, just hang in there," she says.

"Becca!" Rupert manages to say through the pain. "Becca's in trouble, she's in Jason's shed, please save her," he says taking a deep inhale of breath between each word to try and stop the pain. He then hears footsteps coming into the property and Jess shouting to over where Jason is crumpled on the floor.

Rupert's world is becoming blurry and everyone sounds like they are far away. He hears in the distance "Jason Isaac you are under arrest on suspicion of murder. You do not..." It drifts further off into the distance and then he hears Jess's voice. "Stay with me, Rupert, stay with me." And then the world goes black.

Chapter 51

The ambulance was there within a minute of Rupert losing conscious and started prepping him to get him to the hospital. Andrew arrived shortly afterwards and arrested Jason under the suspicion of murder, kidnap and preventing the course of justice. He also needed an ambulance due to the blow that Jess dealt to him. He was knocked out cold. He had just come around when they were rushing Rupert out on a stretcher to the ambulance. He was screaming the place down. "YOU WILL PAY FOR THIS RUPERT! YOU WILL PAY FOR THIS!" He was being strapped to a stretcher shouting, "GET OFF ME! GET OFF ME."

He heard Andrew say to him, "Keep it down." Staying by Rupert's side the entire time in the ambulance, Jess called John. The conversation was brief and to the point. She knew that her team, apart from Andrew, who was heading to Rupert's flat, with her to explain what they had found had headed straight to Jason's house. John picked up straight away. "Hi Jess, Jason's not at the house, we are going through the rooms to determine his location." Jess was struggling to hear him over the sirens but she shouted, "We have him! He's in custody and on his way to the hospital." John starts to speak "Well…"

"Look John," she interrupts. "You need to look in the shed!" The paramedics are putting tubes and cannulas in Rupert and trying to keep his breathing going. They talk to him as they work. "Steady, Rupert, we are almost at the hospital now."

The paramedic grabs the radio in the back of the ambulance

and speaks, "Good afternoon, just wanted to make you aware we are alerting a stabbing, get the crash cart ready and prep for surgery."

Jess, trying to listen to both, speaks to John again, "John did you get that? Check the shed! The sister should be in there get an ambulance and help her."

She hears John shout to David. "David, shed! Now!"

"Keep me updated," Jess says as she puts the phone down and holds Rupert hand. She notices that both of her own hands are stained with his blood. As soon as they arrive to the hospital there is a team waiting for them. They grab Rupert's stretcher and as they rush off, she tries to keep up with them she hears the paramedics relaying all the information to the doctors "This is Rupert Graham, male, mid-thirties, been stabbed in the lower abdomen, his blood pressure is falling." They step up their pace and Jess struggles to keep up as they rush through the double doors and they are gone. Jess is left standing there in silence just praying that Rupert survives it.

Jess decides to call Andrew. The phone starts ringing and she hears his ringtone and turns around to see Andrew walking through the double doors with Jason, both hands cuffed to either side of the bed, he's very quiet and looks zoned out. "They sedated him when we got back into the ambulance," Andrew says to her. "He was kicking off too much. They thought he might do himself some serious damage." Jess is about to say something to Andrew when her phone goes off. It's John. She answers before it's even rang a second time. "Give me some good news, John," she says.

"We have her, the paramedics are just looking over her now. They think she's in a lot of shock but she going to be okay. We are just bringing her in."

Jess sighs in relief and sits down on one the hospital waiting chairs "Oh thank God!" she says, "Thank you, John! See you soon." She puts the phone down. She's overwhelmed with emotion and a tear forms in her eye. Andrew sits down next to her. "Well done, Jess," he says.

"For what? Andrew, a girl has died and two more people almost died because we didn't spot the signs earlier. He sat opposite us in that room Andrew, and neither of us picked up on it."

"Jess! We just saved two people from dying whose time wasn't up yet. We couldn't do anything about. He's a lawyer so he knew what to do to make it more convincing but it was your determination that made the team investigate the shoes and the CCTV, so don't beat yourself up."

Jess who's about to answer is interrupted by the doctor. "Detective?"

She stands up. "Yes," she says.

"I have some news on Rupert Graham, can you follow me?"

Chapter 52

From the darkness a light starts shinning from the distance and Rupert's eyes strain to open as he adjusts the room comes into focus and he sees a hospital ceiling. Then hears the sounds of slow beeping. He goes to sit up but pain shoots through his stomach again and he lays down. Jess enters his vision as she puts her hands on his shoulders. "Whoa, easy there," she says and she sits back down, he turns his head to face her. "It was touch and go there a bit," Jess says. "You had us all worried!"

"Becca?" He says frantically remembering about Becca in the shed. "Is she okay?" He breathes heavily. "Did you find her?"

Jess puts her hands on his bed and says, "Yes, don't worry, she is safe, she's just outside the room. She's been quite insistent that she wants to see you. We've asked her to wait until you had come around," she says.

Rupert immediately relaxes and then asks, "What's happened to Jason?"

"He's currently in this hospital receiving treatment for his head wound but he is under arrest and will be charged with murder, kidnap and perverting the course of justice as soon as we get him to the police station when he is released by the doctors."

Rupert rests his head back down on the pillow and looks down and sees one arm in plaster and a big bandage wrapped round his stomach, he is so relieved that he is still here he really thought he was a goner.

"I'm not going to ask you too many questions because you

need to rest but did he give you any reason why he had done this to you?" Jess asks him. "He said that my ex-wife had told her family that I had cheated several times and I had abused her. He told me he had seen the bruises, which is not true, it's all a lie to protect herself."

"Don't worry, Rupert, I believe you. We have finally been able to make contact with your ex-wife and she is making her way to the station now to make a statement."

"Thank you," Rupert says, "if you hadn't been there before to talk to me you wouldn't have been so close. I would have been dead without a doubt so I can't thank you enough."

"I'm so sorry, Rupert. The chiefs will be livid at me for saying that, but I am, Rupert. He was one step ahead of us all the time and because he was a lawyer, he knew exactly what we needed to hear and how to push us in the right direction and he did a pretty good job at making it airtight. One of our officers missed vital evidence which they will be reprimanded for. Jason had ultimately forgotten about the trainers and the CCTV so we have evidence that puts him at the scene and then with the voicemail."

"He had Becca's phone? He said he had wiped it," Rupert says remembering like a flashback.

"He did and he had wiped it, but fortunately Becca had backed it up at home so we have it safely back at the station."

Rupert shuts his eyes in relief and emotion just floods over him. "Thank you so much," he says, with tears starting to drop down his face. "You don't need to thank me, Rupert. I should have believed you and I'm sorry. I'd better go because otherwise I'm going to get in trouble for stressing you out and I think it's important to rest and heal we have a tough couple of months coming up. As soon as you are well enough we will get to the station to give a statement but take your time. Are you happy for me to allow Becca in?" Jess says.

"Yes of course. Thanks, Jess." he says wiping the tears away from his eyes. "Speak soon, Rupert." She opens the door and nods to Becca who comes rushing in

"Thank god you are okay," Becca says to him as she goes to give him a hug but stops herself after seeing the bandage. Jess shuts the door and Rupert watches her walk down the corridor. Becca and Rupert chat everything through he says sorry over and over until she tells him to stop and that it wasn't his fault. They talk until Rupert falls back to sleep and Becca stays by his side the whole time in hospital.

Chapter 53

Three Months Later

Rupert's sat in his new house. The old flat had too many memories and he needed a fresh start out and that meant leaving the city he had always lived in. He tried to stay there but there were too many looks and whispers and he needed to leave. He's now in a nice seaside town and his house looks out on to the beach.

He had to undergo an extreme two months of physiotherapy to get his strength back in his arm and to be able to build his stomach muscles back up. All while going through the court case. Jess had given the option that he could sit it out and only go when he needed to give testimony but he had insisted that he wanted to be there. When he had arrived and sat down, his eyes caught Jason's, who sat handcuffed. There was still hate there. Jason's lawyer tried to destroy him on the stand, trying to make him out to be a liar and tried to make it sound like he had hired Jason to do the killing for him, as a perverse way of getting satisfaction. Rupert held strong and told his side and kept looking across at the jury every now and then. The court case lasted a month, there was countless evidence brought from both sides although the prosecution had far stronger evidence. Rupert's ex-wife, Steph, came to be a character witness for Jason. She stood on the stand and said how he had been a loving brother and had always looked out for his family. This wasn't him he was just doing what he thought was right for his family. The part that made Rupert sick was that she lied about telling Jason about the multiple affairs and the abuse when questioned, she denied that she had told him that. That's Steph all over, saving her own skin. The waitress and the two women Jason had paid also got done for perverting the course of justice.

The verdict came out yesterday and is now splashed across the paper that Rupert has on his kitchen table. The headline reads KILLER LAWYER GETS LIFE FOR REVENGE KILL. Jason got no chance of bail he will be in prison for the rest of his life and Rupert couldn't be more relieved. It's the best place for him to be.

Rupert's been trying to put back the pieces of his life that Jason ripped apart. His work called him straight away after everything went down and apologised and said they would welcome him back. He had thought about it but decided that he wanted a life and that he decided to change career all together. He's opening his own café on the beach front and feels it's a better move overall. He can get on with his life now. A new chapter. He still sees Becca every now and then. They became friends, united over the situation and kept that togetherness for the court case and beyond. When the verdict was read out in court there was such a relief around the room, he could see it on everyone's face. When they left the court the first person to come up to him was Jess.

She said, "Well done, Rupert," and shook his hand that wasn't in the cast. "That's exactly what that bastard should have got. The world is a safer place now we know he is behind bars."

"Thank you for all you help, Jess, thank goodness we can put it all behind us. I hope you are taking a break after all this," he had said to her.

"Me and my son are going camping next week for a long break I can't wait," she said and with that they shook each other's hand and said their farewells and walked off into different directions. Each of them scarred by what happened but ultimately heading off to better things.

Chapter 54

Do you really think you have gotten away with it, Rupert? You think you have won and think you are safe? Let me tell you, YOU ARE NOT! You may have hurt us this time but we will come back and we will make you pay for what you done to us. Remember you betrayed us and we don't forget. We are going to leave you for a while, we have talked it through and we know what the plan is and boy, are we going to do it better this time. One day not so far in the future you will pay for this when you least expect it. Just. You. Wait!

The End.